Changeling Press. LLC

ChangelingPress.com

The Mermen Duet
Urban Fantasy Romance
Ashlynn Monroe

The Mermen (Duet)
Urban Fantasy Romance
Ashlynn Monroe

All rights reserved.
Copyright ©2024

ISBN: 978-1-60521-900-4

Publisher:
Changeling Press LLC
315 N. Centre St.
Martinsburg, WV 25404
ChangelingPress.com

Printed in the U.S.A.

Editor: Kira Stone
Cover Artist: Angela Knight

The individual stories in this anthology have been previously released in E-Book format.

Table of Contents

Maid for the Mermen (Mermen 1)
Ashlynn Monroe

Couch surfing and temp jobs were a way of life for Daisy Daniels after she aged out of the foster care system. She's always taken life one day at a time and gone with the flow. She never expected that flow would lead her down a raging current of uncertainty about her life and the world she knows.

River, Ocean, and Bayou Waterson need someone to keep their island home neat and tidy, but they have a problem. They can't trust any old cleaning service. They need to find someone who will be willing to overlook their differences. What they never expected was to find a live-in maid they would all love.

When Daisy discovers the celebrity treasure hunters are really mermen, will she be able to keep her head above water? An ancient prophecy brings danger to their doorstep. Forces she never imagined are conspiring to destroy everything that matters to her. The only thing that can save her is a bond she can't break. Saving the world definitely wasn't in the job description.

Chapter One

Daisy Daniels had a hell of a hangover, but that was the price of living her best party life. She tugged the office door open. Ocean View Temporary Workers smelled of musty depression.

"How's it going, Sassy Sally?" Daisy handed Sally a cup of her favorite, Americano with two pumps of hazelnut.

Sally smiled, the crow's feet at the corner of her eyes growing more prominent. "Not bad, Dangerous Daisy," she replied, using the karaoke night nickname earned when Daisy had gotten her long brown braid caught in the DJ's equipment at the bar they liked. "I guess you got my message."

"I did." Daisy sat down in front of Sally's desk. "So, what's this opportunity? I'm enjoying the front desk at Mort's Auto. It's cake. Why would I want something different unless they don't need a temp anymore?" Nervous, Daisy glanced around the room. A few new motivational posters caught her attention. Corporate had really gone all out with kittens this month. She forced herself to look at Sally. "You sounded crazy excited."

"I am." Sally twirled a lock of her long, graying blonde hair.

Daisy frowned. That was Sally's tell move and the reason why she always lost at cards. Daisy's anxiety spiked. "Am I fired or something?"

"Nothing like that," Sally scoffed. The lines on her forehead seemed more noticeable as her normal playful expression became pensive. "You've been couch surfing since you aged out of the system. It's going on three years, honey. You need to figure things out. Temp work is great and all, but wouldn't you like something a little more permanent?"

Honestly, the word *permanent* terrified Daisy. She let go of the breath she'd held. "No."

Sally flinched, scowling. "No?" Her bright blue eyes simmered with hurt. She reached across the desk and took Daisy's hand.

"You heard me." Daisy looked down at the fraying carpet to hide her pain.

Sighing, Sally squeezed Daisy's hand before letting it go. "Will you hear me out before making the decision?"

Daisy glanced up. Sally was the only person she had to rely on. She owed her the respect to at least listen. "Okay, but I don't want you to push me into anything. I know how you are. You want to fix everyone. I'm not broken."

Sally smiled sadly. "Honey, we're all a little broken. Anyway, here's what I've got. Live-in maid for three bachelors in a beach house."

"Ewww! What? Sal?" Daisy was at a loss for a more thorough response.

Sally held up her hands. Her eyes were wide, and desperation crept into her expression. "No, come on, not *ewww*. Think about it. This is perfect."

"How the hell is that perfect?" Daisy had foster families treat her like the help. The last thing she wanted was that crap again. "I'm a slob. And living with three strange dudes sounds sketchy as heck."

"I promise you they aren't creepers." Sally took off her glasses and rubbed the bridge of her nose.

"How can you know for sure?" Daisy crossed her arms over her chest and leaned back in her chair. "This is *not* how I die. I think I've seen this movie. It doesn't end well for the unsuspecting maid!"

Sally sighed as she put her glasses back on. "Don't be so dramatic. I'll send you a thousand YouTube links teaching you to clean. You can learn anything on the Internet. Here -- look at this one." Sally pulled out her phone, swiped, and tapped. She all but shoved the screen in Daisy's face. A woman was giving a tutorial on getting a wine stain out of a white tablecloth.

"Did you have that ready? Like you guessed how I'd react?" Daisy shook her head.

"Don't you give me those sad brown puppy-dog eyes, lady," Sally scolded. "I mean it. You can do *this*. You'd have a roof over your head, meals, and more money than you're making at Mort's. You'd have every Saturday off and a week of paid vacation annually."

"Annually?" Daisy choked on the word.

"Yes, annually. They want someone long-term. They're hiring a temp for a three-month trial basis. If it works out, they'd want the maid to stay on indefinitely."

"Indefinitely?" Daisy squeaked. Her blood ran hot, then cold in her veins. Taking life day-to-day was an adventure. Living with some creepy old dudes as a servant sounded like torture.

"Yes. And you fit the requirements perfectly. They want someone without a spouse or children to live in private quarters on the property. This person would need to sign an NDA, you know, a nondisclosure agreement. The housekeeping and cooking are all you'd have to do. These gentlemen said they want to hire someone who will become part of the family." Sally paused. "Daisy, wouldn't that be nice?"

"No," Daisy said firmly. She didn't look away

from Sally's hopeful gaze. "NDA? Sounds like there's something weird there, and I don't want to end up with some drug dealers or human traffickers. What do these old guys have to hide?"

Sally smiled like a Cheshire Cat. Not a good sign, in Daisy's experience with her friend. She had something up her sleeve and Daisy wasn't sure she was ready for a wild card.

Sally's eyes sparkled with her over-the-top brand of enthusiasm. "The best part is they're famous. Hence the NDA."

"Damn it," Daisy muttered, curious now. "Why didn't you lead with that?"

"I needed you to think about the job, not just the bosses. You know the show I like? *Exploring the Deep*?"

"Of course, you make me watch it with you every Wednesday when I stay at your house --" Daisy stopped as she realized where this was going.

Sally's smile widened until Daisy wondered if her friend would need surgery to fix the perma-grin. "Those three hot hunks are the bachelors in question."

Daisy leaned back in her chair. "Wow. Reality show treasure hunters, interesting. And all I have to do is clean up after them?"

"Yep, and you get a place to stay. If you don't like it, leave in three months with something new on the resume. With the NDA, you probably won't be able to specify who you worked for, but still." Sally waited expectantly.

"Do you only want me to take this job because you're in love with those three?"

"I am not in love with them." Sally's chin rose. "My beloved Benjamin would be very offended."

Sally had been with her on-again off-again boyfriend for twenty-five years.

Daisy thought about having a regular place to stay. She hadn't had one in so long she wasn't sure she could do it. Would she get restless even with such a unique opportunity? Shrugging, she decided to ask a few more questions. "What's the pay like? You said I get to stay, but do I have to pay for the room and food?"

"Oh no, hon. Room and board are included. Just imagine it. You. A private island. All-you-can-eat shrimp. I'm tempted to take the job! *But* you're a lot younger than me. *And* I don't want to break my sweet Benjamin's heart. You're looking at a monthly salary of $3,200. Unfortunately, no health insurance."

Daisy decided three months wouldn't kill her. "Okay, but if they murder me, it's your fault. And you can help me pay the medical bills for machete wounds or chainsaw injuries."

"They won't murder you." Sally scowled. "They'd better not. You're worse at karaoke than I am. I need you to make me sound better. And, of course, I love you."

"Do they actually live around here?" Daisy's brow furrowed. Ocean View was too small of a town to hide celebrities.

"Sort of. They own an island off the coast. And there's one more catch. There isn't any Internet or cell reception." Sally appeared to be holding her breath.

Daisy frowned. "There's always a catch, isn't there?" She started second-guessing saying yes. "Will you be able to check up on me? What if they're some kind of serial killers or perverts or cult members -- I don't know, just something evil?"

"I'll come to check up on you, personally. If you're in danger, just tell me to check on your plants. We both know you don't have any, but they don't know."

Daisy sighed. These guys were famous, and that meant hurting her could ruin their reputation and get their show canceled if word got out. NDA or no NDA, if they tried anything funny she'd go straight to the cops. Maybe it was time to take a chance.

This could be interesting. Celebrities? Definitely not your everyday live-in maid position. Working for these guys did sound kind of cool. Daisy nodded. "Okay. As long as you personally check on me if you don't see me on my day off. People survived without the Internet once upon a time. I guess I can try living like ye olden days before TikTok."

"The boat ride to the island is short. As soon as you hit the mainland, you'll have to signal, or so they've said. They have a satellite phone for emergencies. Will you do it?" Sally looked like a kid waiting to see Santa.

Daisy rolled her eyes. "Yes, fine, I'll be the maid for your idols. But if they're creepy or slobs, I'm out of there in three months and I expect your spare room to be open."

Sally nodded. "For sure. You can crash if this doesn't work out. But this could be great for you. Life on a private beach with a safe, long-term place to sleep. I wish, when I was your age, I'd had this chance."

"When you were twenty-one there wasn't any Internet, so I guess you could say you got half of this fabulous opportunity to be abandoned on an island with TV hunks," Daisy teased.

Sally tossed her pen playfully across the desk. "You're a brat."

Daisy's smile fell away. "Let's hope they don't agree with you. I do love lounging on the beach." But Daisy knew deep down this challenge wasn't going to be all sunshine and sand. In her soul, she could feel the clouds gathering. She hoped she could handle the hurricane something this tricky could turn into.

* * *

Daisy had slept -- more like tossed and turned -- at Sally's the previous night. It felt weird leaving her vehicle behind at the harbor, the rusty hunk of junk being her most valuable possession. She'd been told to bring a bag in case this worked out and she could spend the night settling in. Everything she owned fit into a large suitcase and overnight bag, so she decided to bring it all. After grabbing her pillow, she looked at the small pile on the ground. So little to show for twenty-one years of life. It caused a wave of melancholy to wash over her while locking the car.

She'd looked for the boat called *Siren*. It didn't take long. The huge thing was no boat. This was a yacht. "Wow," she muttered to herself.

"Do you like her?" a male said from behind her.

Daisy jumped, but she didn't look to see who'd asked. "It's pretty. I've never been on a boat before."

"Are you Daisy Daniels?"

When she heard her name, she turned. Her mouth went dry. She'd seen an episode of his TV show with Sally here and there, but she'd always been more interested in playing with her phone than the program. She vaguely recognized this guy as one of the hotties Sally drooled over. He wasn't just TV pretty. This guy was hot. A total hunk. His long black hair, casually tied back in a ponytail, made her a bit envious. He had a black goatee and eyes so brown they could have been black. His skin, tanned, and his upper body, powerful. His arms looked like they belonged to a body builder. She opened her mouth, at a loss for words.

He grinned, as if amused. "You do realize this

job is on an island. The only way off and on is by boat. Are you sure you're up for it?"

Mort's had already replaced her with another temp. She needed this job. Nodding, Daisy dropped her overnight bag and stuck out her hand. "I'm up for it."

"River Waterson." He shook her hand firmly.

Daisy picked up her bag. She couldn't help wondering if it was actually his name or a stage name for his reality show.

"Let me take something for you," River offered. He gave her a tight smile.

"You don't have to do that, Mr. Waterson. It's not heavy." Years of having things stolen made Daisy nervous to hand off her belongings.

"Don't worry, I won't run off with it." He held out his hand. "And please, it's River. Three Mr. Watersons could get a bit confusing."

Daisy nodded. Wanting to seem cooperative and make a good impression, she reluctantly let him take the handle of her suitcase. He rolled it behind him as they approached the boat.

They walked to the dock and then up a wobbly metal ramp. Daisy took hold of the railing, feeling a little woozy.

"Careful. You'll need to get those sea legs if we all agree you're a good fit," River said.

Worry nibbled at the back of her mind. His words reminded her this wasn't a sure thing, but an interview. Whatever happened, she'd just have to figure things out. Silently, she cursed Sally's idea. It wasn't as if Daisy qualified as maid material. These guys would probably see that. At least Sally would be obligated to let Daisy crash at her place.

"Do you have time left on a lease somewhere?"

River asked.

Daisy mentally cursed. She still wasn't totally sure how to frame her lack of permanent address, so she didn't sound flighty. And was this guy some kind of mind reader or just super perceptive?

He helped her down into the yacht. Daisy's eyes widened. "Wow! Is that a pool?"

"It is. But back to my question --"

"Sorry," Daisy accidently interrupted. She was blowing this; she could tell. "I -- I've been staying with a friend. Which is good because I can start working immediately. I don't have kids or a boyfriend. I have no problem signing an NDA."

He grunted as he secured her luggage on deck.

She wondered what they'd been hoping for. Maybe they wanted a grandmotherly type? Then again, these guys were young. Did they want a supermodel with aspirations to become the next Martha Stewart? She bit her lip.

"You can get comfortable." He pointed to some very plush seating above them. "Or if you'd rather, you can go below. We'll be at the island in fifteen minutes. Don't worry, I'm a great captain."

"Thanks. It's so beautiful out here I'll just sit up top." She climbed the stairs and took a seat. A few minutes later they were sailing away from land and modern communications. Daisy hoped she wasn't embarking on a trip to a horror movie where hunks lured young women to die. Shivering, even with the day's warmth, Daisy forced her mind away from the terrible images. She'd spent too many years distrusting people. Instead, she enjoyed the wind in her hair and closed her eyes, letting the sun warm her face. Summer on the Atlantic felt magical. Blue sky and soft, puffy clouds met the ocean to stretch into an infinite horizon.

This was the opportunity of a lifetime… if she didn't screw up the interview.

A coastline came into view. Daisy stood up to see better. The island looked amazing. Dense trees gave the land privacy, but she could see the glittering of windows on the far side of the island as they got closer. Daisy realized from the mainland all anyone could see was the natural vegetation. These guys must really like privacy. Worry crept back again, but she pushed her fear away.

When they reached the dock, River busied himself with mooring the yacht. Daisy took the moment to get a look at her surroundings. The island wasn't small. A sandy beach stretched into a manicured lawn leading up into the clearing where an enormous house rose imposingly over the ocean. It appeared modern. The glass windows sparkled in the sun, yet a gothic creepiness dampened Daisy's wonder. The building stood big and modern, but its cold loneliness would have lent substance to a Bronte novel. She couldn't even swim. It was too late to watch how he turned on the engine and steered the boat. Glancing around she looked for anything she could defend herself with if needed. She wasn't going down without a fight.

"Second thoughts?" River asked, standing behind her.

Daisy jumped. She paused. "Not really."

"Okay, if you're sure you want to continue the interview, we'll go meet the others."

He seemed far too perceptive. She tried to keep her expression blank.

River helped Daisy out of the boat. She noticed they left her bags. She had the feeling River Waterson had made up his mind about her. The feeling made her dislike him a bit.

River chuckled.

"What's so funny?" Sure, she wasn't an expert boater, but he didn't have to laugh at her awkward disembarking. *Rude.*

"I'm not laughing at you." He led her up the sandy beach.

"Are you a mind reader?"

River stopped abruptly giving her such an intense look she had to push down her heightened sense of self-preservation. She wanted to run from him. But she couldn't. She needed this job. It wasn't like he'd be around her all day as she cleaned up. She'd probably never see him if she got this job. Nothing about the way he looked at her made sense. Nothing about the way his look made her feel made sense. There was just something about him. Something she couldn't put a finger on.

Straightening her back, she drew on every ounce of courage she possessed and looked him straight in the eyes.

His brow furrowed. "Of course not. You just have a very expressive face. There's nothing to fear. You're safe on this island."

She shrugged. Maybe she'd made her apprehension too obvious. The guy was a celebrity. He'd probably spent years watching his back. And she had a terrible poker face. She'd lost her shirt, literally, the last time someone had asked her to play.

He chuckled again. Her uneasiness returned as she trudged up the beach and into the grass. It became easier to make it up the embankment once they were out of the sand. The tangy air blew the cool ocean breeze around her. Sand, surf, and trees surrounded her with picture perfect beauty. Sally was right, this was the chance of a lifetime. She hadn't had a place to call home most of her life. A temporary arrangement like this could be a good test. If she couldn't make a private island feel like home, she'd never be more than a nomad. Roots, even ones she'd have to transplant eventually, might be nice. None of the foster homes had ever felt… right.

"Follow me," River said.

He turned and instead of going to the massive house, they went to a bungalow. The smaller building matched the larger house.

"Cute." Daisy stopped to admire the flower boxes on the windows. Geraniums in pink, white, and red grew robustly.

"This is the cottage. If you're offered the job, and accept it, you'll live here." River opened the door.

She followed him inside. The little house had a full kitchen and living area all in a nautical theme. A TV hung on the wall. River opened a door on the left. The bedroom housed a big, four-poster bed. White scarves wrapped around the posts. She also saw a full bathroom adjoining the bedroom. "This is nice." Daisy could totally see herself living here.

"There's satellite television service, but we don't have Internet or a reliable cell phone connection."

"I'd been warned. I can live without it. Why didn't you get satellite Internet?" She'd done without cell phones and computers most of her life. Foster parents, at least the ones she'd had, weren't into paying for those amenities.

Shrugging, River frowned. "We tried it, but the signal was so slow we decided to cancel. It's nice, in a way. We get more peace than everyone else. There isn't a constant need to respond to emails and messages."

Daisy didn't have many people who emailed or

messaged her anyway. She would miss zoning out to random stuff on YouTube. "I still want to take the job."

River nodded. "It's time you met the others."

Daisy's heart gave a painful beat as her anxiety returned. Nerves made her palms sweat. Maybe she could charm the rest. River barely seemed to like her. She had no idea how to be charming.

River chuckled. He walked ahead of her so she couldn't see his face.

She frowned. He seemed to time his amusement with her crazy thoughts. Or maybe she just always thought ridiculous stuff and it was a coincidence.

He chuckled again.

She shivered and could only hope mystery laughter wasn't a trait they all shared.

Chapter Two

Daisy followed River up the small knoll onto the vast lawn surrounding the massive house. She'd call the place a mansion. Sunlight glittered off the big windows, giving it a magical quality as the tangy sea breeze and beauty made it less gothic and imposing. The quiet feeling of being in such an obscure place only added to the distortion of reality, making her feel like they were the only people on the planet.

River didn't turn around to look at her. "Bayou and Ocean are waiting. They're excited to meet you. But I'll give you a tour first."

Was he just being nice? Famous people had to know more exciting people than "the help".

Daisy stood in awe as she entered the enormous house. "Wow. This place is spotless." Then she remembered she'd have to keep it this clean.

River led her through the foyer and down a hallway. They passed several rooms that looked like offices. "We have a lot of meetings here. The offices only require you to clean the floors and do some light dusting. Never move any of the objects or paperwork. And Bayou is a bit territorial, so his office is completely off limits." River pointed to a closed door. "When we have a meeting in the big meeting room, we'd like to make sure it's spotless so feel free to bring me any paperwork or items left behind when you clean it. We'll let you know when we need it seen to. There's a list we'll provide you of the amenities we want to make sure are well stocked. We need coffee, water, snacks, notebooks, pens, tissues, and such available so there's no reason for long breaks. The agency told you

you'll need to cook too, right?"

Oh God, what had Sally gotten her into? "Umm, yes," she lied. Daisy could make an amazing boxed macaroni and cheese dinner when necessary, but she wasn't a gourmet chef.

River chuckled his infuriating chuckle. "We don't need anything fancy, but we like to eat clean and healthy. You'll oversee making sure meals are delivered for the number of meeting attendees. Any allergies or dietary restrictions will be included in the information you'll be given before any meetings. We get a delivery of items from the mainland weekly. You can add anything you desire to the list, but remember we can't just run you back to shore on a whim so plan accordingly."

Daisy remained silent as she followed him, overwhelmed and suddenly a little insecure. She'd never seen such a huge kitchen. What seemed like infinite cabinets stretched across the blue and white mosaic tiled walls. A hanging rack filled with pans hung over an impressive center island. Everything appeared perfectly pristine. Fresh flowers sat on a small breakfast table in a sunny nook.

Daisy swallowed around the lump in her throat and fought the feeling she'd desecrate this hallowed space with her lack of culinary expertise by just standing in the doorway. Most of the foster homes she'd lived in hadn't even had stoves with four working burners. She'd learned to cook out of the necessity of hunger, not the luxury of enjoyment. No one had ever taken time to show her how to navigate the domestic side of life like a normal person. Surviving had been enough for her then. Now she wished someone had given her a little more. But *more* was a dangerous thing. Wanting only left a void.

Getting through the day unscathed needed to be enough. *Enough* brought comfort.

River looked at Daisy, studying her face. She noticed his gaze when she turned to tell him she wasn't the right person for this job. He seemed almost sad. "You strike me as someone who hasn't had an easy life. We don't have unreasonable expectations. Anyone can learn just about anything. We knew we were getting a local person from a small town, not a big city chef. What matters is loyalty and trust."

Far too insightful, as usual, he made her want to try. Daisy's throat tightened. "I appreciate your honesty. I can only promise to do my best and uphold your privacy and the rules outlined in the NDA." If he meant what he said, she'd give this maid business a try. What did she have to lose?

River nodded, once and firmly. "Good. Now let me show you the rest of the house, and then you can meet my family." He left the kitchen and she followed him into a large dining room. When Sally had gifted her with a book on table settings and etiquette she'd laughed. Now she couldn't be more grateful. A massive chandelier hung over a table that could easily accommodate twenty. How many boxes of mac and cheese would she need for those parties?

River smiled. "We don't entertain much. No need for food calculations today."

He really was spooky. The weirdest part, Daisy found the mind reading comforting and disturbing in equal measure. He allayed her fears the moment they crept into her head. Maybe she should ask him for the winning lottery numbers for this week's drawing? "Probably for the best, I suck at doing math in my head."

This time, when he laughed, she didn't have the

same level of creep out. He was good looking -- when he wasn't scowling.

He scowled.

Daisy bit her lip. Even if he had a talent for reading people, she sensed she'd put the expression on his face with her assessment somehow. She needed to work on keeping her expression neutral. Sally always said Daisy couldn't have resting bitch-face because her face never stayed still long enough to rest. She'd never been someone to hide her emotions. Which was probably what scared off every guy who ever tried to stick around. She couldn't think of River as handsome or male. He was her new boss, maybe, and as such totally off limits. Screw herself out of a good thing by screwing him? Nope.

"This way," he said after he cleared his throat.

Was he blushing?

Daisy's eyes narrowed, but he didn't give her time to get a good look at his face. She followed him up a curved staircase. The dark wood gleamed. "This is amazing."

"Thank you," he replied. "Ocean carved it himself."

"Wow. I wish I had a talent." She touched the cool wood. "It's art."

"Wait until you see his room." River led her upstairs. There was a large open area with chairs and a floor to ceiling bookshelf filled with a wide variety of books.

Daisy couldn't help wondering if they were for show or if these guys were the quiet-Friday-night-reading-at-home types.

"These are our shared volumes, but we all have our personal favorites."

Not just for display then. A bit of a bookaholic

herself, the revelation made her glad she'd have something in common with these guys. Daisy followed him to the first closed door.

"Please don't do anything more than light dusting and the floors in our bedrooms. We will leave our personal laundry in the hall on Monday morning. Make sure each of us gets his own clothing back. This is my room."

Everything in the room stood as perfect as the rest of the house. Daisy nodded. The least she could do was ensure her employers weren't wearing another man's underwear. Against her better judgment, her eyes drifted to River's sculpted backside as he closed the door and she followed him. Those pants made his ass look spectacular.

He cleared his throat again, and she quickly raised her gaze to his back. Which didn't help much because she noticed just how wide his shoulders were. His upper body appeared powerful, but that made sense since he did so much diving. Or at least his show made it seem that way.

Her traitorous brain flashed back to the bits of the damn show. *Curse you, Sally*! Her mind's eye stayed wide open, ogling River's six pack abs as he dove off his side of his boat. *Uuuggghhh*! What red blooded straight woman would blame her for the sudden spike in her overactive libido? Didn't they get some magazine's sexiest something award?

The second and final time they'd taken her away from Mom, a kind social worker had whispered doing math in her head would help her stop crying. Would the trick also help keep her from a totally lust melt down? *One plus one is two, two plus two is four, the square root of…*

"This is Bayou's room. You do not have to do

anything with the tanks."

Inside were at least a dozen fish tanks. The variety of aquatic life amazed her. Everything appeared clean and the creatures seemed healthy. He didn't have much else in the room beside a bed. If she got to know him, she'd love to learn about the animals he kept. She'd never had a pet, not even a fish.

"Bayou likes to keep to himself. He's not very… communicative."

Daisy thought about the handful of episodes she'd seen of their reality show. River did most of the talking. Ocean featured prominently on the screen but not Bayou. He always seemed to be doing grunt work in the background.

River snorted as he shut the bedroom door. "We all work very hard for the life we have, and no one is superior to another in our family."

Daisy shrugged. It wasn't her business, but she'd remember to be extra kind to Bayou and give him whatever space he required.

"How are you guys all related again?" Daisy followed him farther down the hall.

"We're cousins."

River opened another door.

Daisy's mouth dropped. "Wow! This is amazing." She couldn't help herself, touched to the core of her soul, as she stepped inside the room. The space looked like it could be the cabin of a pirate captain. It struck her as so beautiful she had to fight the urge to cry for some inexplicable reason. The feeling, indescribable.

"Take a look out the window," River said softly.

She startled, having been so caught up in the room she'd almost forgotten her guide was right there in the doorway. She stepped over to one of the tall windows -- different from any of the others in the house -- and looked out. Her breath caught in her throat. Emotion suffocated her for a moment before she got herself under control again. "It feels like I'm sailing."

"When we had the house built, Ocean knew this was exactly what he wanted. We had his room built suspended over the water. The windows and room are a reproduction of the captain's quarters from *Queen Anne's Revenge*."

Daisy briefly remembered one of the few episodes she'd seen of the show showing her potential employers exploring the wreck. "Wasn't that Blackbeard's ship? And the wreck is here in America?"

"North Carolina. Our first gig was with the private research firm who found her. We went solo a few years later, then the History channel offered us the show and here we are today."

"That's cool." She turned to look at him so he could see her face. "I don't think I've found the magical thing that will fulfill my life yet." She turned back to the amazing view.

"You will," he said with such confidence she turned back to him.

"You think so?"

"I do." He shrugged. "Now that you've seen the house, come back downstairs with me to meet the rest of the family.

Nerves fluttering in her belly caused her breath to catch.

"You'll be fine."

She only gave him a tense smile, hoping he was right but knowing he was wrong.

Chapter Three

When they went downstairs, River led her to a patio sitting just off the kitchen. Daisy hadn't seen the door during her first tour of the space. Outside, the patio was as perfect as the rest of the house. Potted flowers and plants gave a sense of privacy even though the yard stretched down to blend into a sandy beach which ended at the ocean. Daisy took a deep breath of the brisk sea air before looking at the other two men who might become her employers.

Bayou and Ocean were as hot as River, but both seemed to have different reactions to her.

Ocean's eyes widened just a bit, almost imperceptibly. He seemed to be studying her carefully, and when their eyes met he smiled. Daisy smiled back. A strange tingle of recognition made her shiver even through the day's warmth.

River exchanged a look with Bayou, who shrugged.

River cleared his throat. "Daisy, these gentlemen are Bayou and Ocean Waterson."

Ocean had overly long blond hair. He looked between River and Daisy before his blue eyes gazed into hers with curiosity now.

Bayou sat back. Daisy could tell he was the tallest of the men, even sitting. His hazel eyes and shaggy dark brown hair gave him a gothic kind of appeal. He almost looked upset that she stood there. A palpable sense of the introvert in him seemed to rebel against welcoming a stranger into his space and made Daisy feel off-kilter. She'd remember to be sensitive to his need for solitude.

"It's nice to meet you," she said, softly. "River has given me a basic idea of what you guys expect, but do either of you have any specific requests?"

Ocean grinned. "Since you've gotten this far, no."

Daisy didn't know what he meant.

"Stay out of my room," Bayou said.

Daisy nodded in his direction. "Sure. I'll pick up the laundry at the door, otherwise I'll stay away from your room. Any other things I should know?"

Bayou shrugged.

"Anything new takes time," River said, looking at Bayou. "He doesn't mean to come off as an asshole. He's a great guy once you get to know him."

"Sure, no worries," Daisy assured him. "I'm just here to do my job. It's totally fine."

"It's not," Ocean said. "We're looking for someone who can work here long-term. I don't want you to get the wrong idea about any of us."

"I'll sign the NDA and it includes this conversation. Don't worry, I'd never say or do anything to affect your public image negatively."

"That's good," River said. "But I get a pretty good read on people. Let's call it a special skill, and I think if you're willing to give us a chance, we'd like to give you one too."

"Does this mean I have the job?" Daisy couldn't believe her good fortune. "I'll do my best."

"That's all we're asking of you. Bayou, could you go down to the boat and put her bags in the cottage?"

Bayou nodded.

"I can get it. I don't want to put you out," Daisy said quickly. She didn't want to give Bayou any additional reasons to dislike her.

"It's fine," Bayou said gruffly. He stood up and

started down to the boat.

She'd been right, he was the tallest, and lanky too. *I hope my cooking doesn't make the poor guy gaunt.*

River chuckled.

Ocean looked over at him. "Later?"

River nodded. "Later."

What's that about? She was a little envious. It'd be nice to have someone know her so well they could have an entire conversation with just one word. Her life had never had a consistent person in it until Sally. *Sally.* Her heart ached a little. *When will I see my Sassy Sally again?*

"We'll be going to the mainland on Friday," River said. "So, you'll get four days of isolation before a trip back to town."

Again, she found his timing strangely comforting. "Thank you. With such a beautiful and big house to take care of, I'm sure the time will fly by."

"Sit down with us." Ocean extended his hand toward the vacant chair. "We can get to know you a little better."

Daisy sat. "It's pretty here."

River sat down on what looked like some kind of outdoor storage box.

"What appealed to you about this job?" Ocean asked.

Daisy didn't know what to say. "A paycheck, I guess. I'm grateful for the generous compensation you're offering."

"We believe in treating our staff well," Ocean said. "Loyalty is priceless, and you don't get it being stingy with the people who help you."

Daisy felt her throat tighten, but she wasn't sure why. Maybe because she'd gotten some rough temp jobs over the last couple of years. "Nice sentiment. I'll do my best to earn your trust. I promise to work hard."

"We've given her the job. Don't treat this like a second interview." River glared at his cousin.

"You're right. I'm sure this is already a bit overwhelming for you. What do you like to do for fun?" Ocean's easy smile returned.

Daisy shrugged one shoulder. "I actually read a lot. But karaoke nights are my favorite. My friend Sally and I go twice a week."

"Do you sing well?" Ocean asked.

Daisy chuckled. "Nope. In fact, I get a free drink if I promise to go toward the end of the night to clear the place out."

River laughed, and this time it wasn't creepy. "We can add honesty to your resume."

"Then why do you like it?" Ocean's brow creased a little.

"Because I got to know some fun people there. It's just a great way to kill time." She'd never thought about the why.

"Unfortunately, we don't have a karaoke machine," Ocean said.

"Let's call that fortunate. I'd hate to get fired for chasing you off your own island with my rendition of *Bohemian Rhapsody* or *Shallow*. Queen and Lady Gaga should sue me." Daisy wanted to ask him questions too but wasn't sure if he'd take offence.

"Ask us any questions you might have," River said.

Daisy nodded, but she wasn't taking any chances. Safer to let them lead. She'd learned by her second foster home to sit back and watch how a household worked before making any assumptions something was or wasn't okay.

"It's understandable to be nervous," River said.

"We're your new employers, after all. Take all the time you need to feel safe here."

Daisy's breath caught in her throat. *Safe.* Horrified, she felt tears prickling behind her eyes. She started doing math in her head quickly. "Thanks." Even to her own ears her voice sounded strained.

"What book are you reading?" Ocean asked, clearly trying to break the sudden tension.

Daisy felt her face heat. Did she lie or tell them the embarrassing truth? They were eventually bound to see her lounging on the beach in her off time with a novel. "*The Pirate's Sexy Lover.*" She waited for a reaction.

"I like Monroe Ashdale's books." Ocean grinned.

Daisy hadn't taken him for a fan of tawdry romances. At least they had something in common. Her cheeks cooled. "Which one is your favorite?"

"*A Pirate's Revenge*," Ocean admitted.

"I liked that one too. The story was with Lady Veronica, right?" She couldn't help being a little suspicious of him.

"Nope. Lady Margaret."

Oh my gosh, real deal, he did read it. Daisy smiled widely. "If you'd like, I can lend you the book when I finish?"

Ocean's eyes seemed to darken a little, maybe it was just the afternoon light fading, but they were even more beautiful with a tint of gray. "I'll take you up on the offer."

Bayou returned. "Everything is inside. When is she sending for the rest of her stuff?"

Daisy felt her flush return. "Um, that's everything."

"Living simply is admirable," River said quickly, pinning Bayou with a look.

Daisy wasn't sure what that was about. "Thanks for bringing my stuff up."

Bayou grunted. "I'm going to my room."

What did I do wrong? Daisy hated starting out on such rough footing with a new boss.

"Don't mind him. It's his way," River said. "We ate before I went to pick you up, but if you're hungry please feel free to have anything in the kitchen. When we go to the mainland you can purchase whatever you'd like for yourself at the cottage."

"Thanks, I am a little hungry."

"Tomorrow morning, meet us in the kitchen at 8 AM. Here's a key for the house as well as the cottage." Ocean handed her a small key ring. "We can give you a more detailed task list and you can start work."

Daisy nodded. "Sounds good."

"Now go inside and grab some food," River ordered as both he and Ocean stood in a gentlemanly fashion.

Daisy took her cue to go. She went back inside and made a sandwich. She also grabbed two bottles of water out of the fridge before going out the patio door. They watched her as she headed to the cottage. *It could've been worse. I could have torn my shorts or fallen off the boat with my luck.* She could have sworn she heard River laughing.

* * *

Ocean cleared his throat as soon as he knew sure the new maid wouldn't hear. "What was so funny?"

River grinned. "A lot. Her mind is open. She's not one for artifice. She was worried she'd starve poor Bayou to death."

"So, she can't cook? Can she clean?" Ocean's eyes narrowed. The other candidates for the job hadn't even made it onto the boat.

"She doesn't think so." River shrugged.

"And why did you decide we should hire her?" Ocean sighed. "You're the mind reader. She's a pretty woman, but we're not paying for looks. Aerwyna can't come back here every week to clean up after us anymore. She has her duties. She might be your sister, but she's not cut out for coming this close to land regularly. Once she takes her vows she may never get to come visit again."

River let out a long sigh. "You're right. She's definitely not adaptable to human culture. It's cute when she tries. I just wish she didn't have to be the one sacrificed to the Aegeans. She's too free of a spirit."

"I know how you feel. I only had brothers, but if my sister was being asked to do it, I'd have tried to talk her out of it." Ocean put his hand on River's arm.

River jerked back. "I don't need you to use *Gift* on me. I'll survive. I did try." He paused, scowling darkly. "But once Aerwyna makes up her mind there's no changing it. She wants to unite the mer."

"The bastard is just completely unworthy." Ocean had always thought of Aerwyna as the baby sister he'd never had. "He's still obsessed with humans destroying themselves."

"I know. Humans have been doing a good job of destroying themselves lately. If the Aegeans continue manipulating them, mer-kind might not survive. Father is torn over her choice. To have a system of safe current worldwide would be amazing for our people."

Ocean nodded. "Her sacrifice would make life easier for those with Pacific ties and trade. But I wish it could be anyone other than Kai."

"Me too." River's eyes darkened.

Ocean ran his hand through his hair. "Back to our first human housekeeper. What made you pick her?"

"She's sad." River rubbed his temples. "But also, strong. There's an inner strength she called on she wasn't even conscious of. I believe she wants this job, and we can trust her. She wasn't here because of who we are. She came to us because of what she needs. That's something we can use to protect our secrets."

* * *

Ocean nodded. River's reasoning made a sort of twisted sense. Ocean studied his prince and dearest friend. "Can you imagine how angry our fathers would be? A human living with the heir is the last thing they'd imagined when they agreed to let us understand this world better."

Closing his eyes Ocean imagined the pretty young maid in the throes of passion under him. Under River. Sharing was something that anyone not part of a Mer Triad couldn't imagine. The image of them pleasuring the human and in turn feeling the echo of her passion was the pinnacle of what the Triad was meant to provide them. The act of sharing was the highest love and respect they could give each other. But Daisy was very human, and her service was needed. This wasn't going to be more than a business arrangement. Unfortunately.

"I haven't decided what I'm going to do," River said sharply. "I don't know if I'll ever be ready to rule Atlantis. It was never supposed to be my destiny, but when my older brother died Father insisted I prepare. The crown has always been too heavy for me."

"And I'm the last one who would push you to make the choice. Whatever you decide you know Bayou and I will be at your side. Triad always. Our life forces are tied to yours until we die."

"Triad always," River agreed. "Becoming king

with an established Triad of past -- traitors -- I would never put either of you in danger." River paused, and sadness passed over his features. "I know the truth about what was done to both of you. I know you're both good men." He ran his hand through his hair. "Daisy is right for the job. I don't sense any selfish motivation behind why she's here. She's had real darkness touch her past, and yet there is light inside her."

"I trust you." Ocean owed River everything, and the prince had never let him down. He'd give his life for him.

"I know. I wonder how Bayou is doing. He has to be terrified of touching her."

Ocean nodded. "And if it happens, how would we explain it? Did you even ask if she has any phobias?"

"That's not exactly a typical interview question."

"But in our case, it's important."

River sighed. "Yeah, but for now, let's see how this goes. Multiple days of isolation might be more than she can handle."

"I was hoping for some good human cuisine," Ocean grumbled. "I'm getting sick of Bayou's traditional menu."

"Sometimes I think the only reason you agreed to come to land with me was to eat." River grinned. "But then I remember your thoughts."

A weight in Ocean's chest made it hard for him to draw a breath. "This was never anything I'd imagined, and more than I could have hoped for."

River put his hand on Ocean's shoulder. "And there wasn't a more deserving male in the kingdom."

Ocean wanted to live up to his prince's expectations, but considering they weren't going home anytime soon he refused to worry about it. It's not like the next princess of Atlantis would swim up to the beach. "Let's go check on Bayou."

They both stood to go inside.

"I do think," River began, but hesitated. "She'd be kind about his affliction."

Ocean snorted. "I'm fascinated. How did you come to this conclusion? There are grown men who are terrified of Bayou. A tiny little lander like her would swim all the way to shore the moment she sees him for what he is."

River chuckled. "She can't swim."

"You are fucking kidding me, right?"

"No."

Ocean didn't even know what to say. "And she still wants to be stranded on an island with us?"

"In a few days we'll know if she can handle us."

"I bet you the pearls you planned to give Aerwyna on her commitment day the maid won't make it to day four."

"You aren't planning to sabotage our chances of keeping her on the payroll, are you? And her name is Daisy. You might as well just accept she's here. I didn't know you hated landers like Bayou does."

"You know I find them useful, for the most part. I just don't think she has it in her."

"You haven't touched her yet. What makes you so sure?"

Ocean gave a half smile. "I've seen what a slob you are, your majesty."

River rolled his eyes, and they went inside.

Chapter Four

Daisy arrived for her first day of work promptly at eight. Ocean stood waiting for her in the foyer.

"Good morning," he said. "Ready?"

Daisy nodded.

Ocean turned and started walking toward the kitchen. Daisy followed him in silence.

River sat at the table by the window.

Daisy noticed what he was eating didn't look like a normal breakfast. "Is that sashimi?"

River looked away from her. "Not exactly."

What he ate wasn't any of her business.

"We'd like you to have breakfast ready each morning by eight, if you're willing to start early," Ocean said, making what they ate her business anyway.

"I can. What do you guys normally eat?" She really hoped it wasn't some kind of sushi.

"Any kind of land -- typical breakfast food," Ocean said. "Except Bayou. He'll make himself something."

Daisy nodded. "Would you like something now?"

Ocean shook his head. "I ate. At lunch we usually have something quick and light. Dinner is our largest meal of the day."

Daisy nodded again. "What do you like?"

"Start with what you enjoy cooking, and we'll go from there," River injected. "I left a task list on the counter."

Ocean seemed surprised. He went over to the list and looked at it, then he glanced at River before sighing. "Are you sure this is it, your majesty?"

Daisy chuckled.

Ocean flushed. "Um, inside joke."

"I assumed as much," Daisy said. "You guys seem close."

"You have no idea," Ocean replied.

His words had weight. Daisy paused. "It's nice. I can't imagine having that."

Ocean gave an uncomfortable grunt as he handed her the list.

"There isn't much on a regular basis." River explained. "We hire a company to do the exterior windows twice a year. We only expect a deep clean once a month. This list is the normal daily tasks. The rest of your time is your own."

Daisy looked over the chores. The amount of work seemed much less than she'd expected. Such a short daily list almost made her suspicious. Why would they want a live-in maid if this is all they wanted? The weird thing on the list was privacy during the evening news. "This is very manageable. Thank you. I do have a question."

"Sure," River said. "What's not clear?"

"Privacy during the news. Do you want me to go to the cottage? If I have more work to finish, can I return at six when the news is over? Or is it just the local news you want privacy for?"

"You can work anywhere but the den." River's tone turned firm. "We have a long tradition of spending the hour together. We watch both the local and national news each night."

Daisy pressed her lips together and tried not to giggle. These guys were so weird. She liked it. There was something nice about them having current events bonding time. She was just glad they hadn't demanded she watch with them. News gave her anxiety. Better for her not to know who had nukes trained on them or how many lives were being snuffed out arbitrarily by the cruelty of fate. Not that Daisy believed in fate.

River picked up his plate and started toward the sink. Daisy set the list down and hurried over to take the dish from him. "Please, let me."

He shrugged as he let her take it. "Do you have any questions?"

"No. Thank you."

"Certainly," River replied. "We'll leave you to your work."

Daisy watched them go toward the offices. She hoped she'd be able to do this. She hadn't had such a great night's sleep in her life. The sound of the ocean outside had been a lullaby. This job happened to be good for her. She rinsed the plate and put it in the dishwasher before picking up her list again.

"Okay, today is the floor. I wonder what I should make for lunch." She started searching the pantry and cupboards. They didn't have an overwhelming amount of ingredients, but they did have things she knew she could use. She grinned, glad Sally had snuck a few cookbooks into her bags. She'd found them when she unpacked last night. *Cooking for Dummies* was a bit offensive, albeit apt.

River's list even included where things were. She went to the hall closet to find the vacuum, mop, and broom. She started sweeping the kitchen when she heard the patio door open. Her back to the door, she assumed it was Bayou coming for breakfast. "What would you like to eat?"

"Humans," said a lovely feminine voice.

Daisy startled and turned. The woman standing there could only be described as incredible. Her long reddish-brown hair had pearls and shells woven into the tresses hanging in waves down to her knees. She wore a skimpy red bikini showing off a photoshopped-perfect figure. One of her new bosses had a hot girlfriend. She hadn't heard any boats. Had this beauty spent the night?

"Hi," was all Daisy managed. Next to the gorgeous visitor, her bun under a kerchief, jeans, and T-shirt were a desecration of fashion.

"People joking, ha, I am funny," said the stranger, awkwardly. She had an accent Daisy couldn't place. It didn't surprise her that famous hunks had an exotic hottie stashed away on their private island.

"Sure," Daisy diplomatically agreed. "I'm the new housekeeper." She stuck out her hand. "I'm Daisy."

"Hello, Flower Lander. I'm Aerwyna." Aerwyna stuck out her hand too instead of shaking Daisy's.

Is she a sex-bot or an alien or something? Geesh, I guess when you're pretty you can get away with being weird. Daisy shook Aerwyna's hand. The woman's eyes widened, and she pulled away. *Rude. I guess pretty on the outside doesn't make you pretty on the inside.* Or maybe she was just really foreign. Daisy suffered a moment of shame over her assumptions. "Sorry," Daisy said. "I hope the handshake didn't offend you."

"Oh, yes, handshake. Ha, a friendly greeting. Thank you for friending me, lander."

"Um, you're welcome," Daisy mumbled. Sex-bot Girl kind of creeped her out. "I didn't realize the Watersons had company. Would you like me to make you some breakfast that's not Soylent Green?"

"I have never tried your human soiled greens. Do they taste like vegetable?"

"Soylent Green, like the old movie where they

find out the government has been feeding people, um people. Sorry, bad joke. Your accent is beautiful. What kind of breakfast food do you enjoy, where you're from?" Daisy hoped to get a little more information about sex-bot without overstepping her place and asking.

"I enjoy fish and the vegetable of the sea. I do like human toast from French."

This chick says human -- a lot. Sex-bot's not-suspicious-at-all programming could use some new code. "Do you mean seaweed? I saw a bunch of packages in different flavors in the cupboard. I can make French toast. Which would you like?"

"I will eat the toast from French. You are a good human housekeeper. I was worried my brother would pick one not as good as me." Aerwyna sat down at the breakfast table and looked out at the ocean, twirling a shell-bedazzled lock of hair.

"So which Mr. Waterson is your brother?" Daisy asked. If she had to guess it would be Bayou. He also seemed socially awkward. None of her new employers had any kind of accent. They all had the same TV perfect pronunciation making her sure they weren't native to the state.

"The prince, of course." Aerwyna still gazed out the window.

Aerwyna must be in on the whole "your majesty" joke. "Right, his majesty River, got it. Where did you guys grow up?" Daisy burned with curiosity. Even if she was just the help there was no way she could hold back *that* question.

Aerwyna motioned out the window with a limp wrist letting her hand just flop around. She started to hum, still not looking at Daisy. Maybe the poor woman had some kind of brain injury? She wished River had disclosed his sister lived with them, and she had issues. The knowledge would have helped her be more sensitive. Caregiving didn't make this a deal breaker.

Daisy went to the fridge and took out some eggs and butter. Then she found cinnamon and vanilla. Once she finally discovered where they kept the bread, she went to work mixing and frying up the "toast from French". When the first few slices were done, she found some syrup and fruit spread in the refrigerator and brought a plate and the toppings over to the table. "The butter was in the fridge. Would you like me to melt some for your French toast?"

Aerwyna turned her attention from the view to look at the food. Her joyful smile appeared sweet. "But-ter?"

Oh my God. The poor woman must suffer so much. Daisy had known a girl with brain trauma in foster care with her. She had fallen from her bike at seven years old. After hitting her head she'd forgotten how to walk. Her parents had given her up into the system when they couldn't deal with her needs. Maybe this poor beauty had forgotten what butter was. "I'll just go get you some. I promise it'll make the French toast tastier."

Aerwyna kept on smiling as she stared out the window but nodded.

Daisy nuked a couple pats of butter and helped Aerwyna put some on the French toast. She put a little syrup on one slice and the fruit spread on the other when Aerwyna just sat looking at the bottles with confusion.

Daisy carefully cut up the pieces. "Would you like a little help?" she asked gently, when Aerwyna skipped the fork and popped a sticky piece right into her mouth with her fingers.

"No!" Aerwyna said sharply as she picked up a second piece. After she'd eaten that one, she smiled again. "You are very good human housekeeper. Very good toast. Brother will like this food." She then proceeded to gobble down the rest with her fingers. Syrup and fruit spread dripped all over her chin and the table. Daisy's heart warmed for her. She felt for River too. He probably spent a lot of time looking out for his sister. The NDA and her light task list made more sense. It wasn't just his show he was protecting. She wasn't qualified as a caregiver, but she'd do her best.

When the last of the food was gone Daisy took a clean cloth and wet it well with warm water. "Would you like some more?"

Aerwyna shook her head.

"May I help get the sticky stuff off?" Daisy asked softly.

Aerwyna frowned.

Daisy gently picked up her hand and started to wipe off her fingers. Aerwyna grinned. It didn't take long to have her clean.

"Very good cleaning of me," Aerwyna said. "I wanted to see. Tell brother hello." Aerwyna got up. "Back to the ocean for me."

Daisy panicked. "Are you sure that's a good idea?" Keeping a sister from drowning hadn't been on the list of chores, but she still felt responsible.

Aerwyna's laugh sounded slightly deranged. It reminded Daisy of a dolphin's trill.

Before Daisy could stop her, she stood up and went out the door. Daisy dropped the cloth on the table and rushed toward the office River had indicated as his. She knocked hard on the wood.

River opened the door and looked down at her

with a surprised scowl.

"Your sister is going into the ocean. I wasn't sure if that's okay. I didn't see a caregiver around."

"Sister?"

"Aerwyna?" *Don't tell me she's a crazy stalker or homeless stranger or something after I fed and cleaned her. This is just my kind of luck.*

"Yes." River said carefully. "Yes. My. Sister. Yeah, um, yes." *Oh God, is he reverting to whatever weird foreign place they're from or do they both have head injuries?*

"Yes, um head injuries," he began. "Her head injury was just terrible. But she's an amazing swimmer, and the doctors say it's the best therapy for her."

"You're just going to let that poor girl go into the ocean unattended? I could go watch her." Daisy bit her lip. *I can't even swim. What would I do if she were drowning? But someone must help the poor woman.*

"No. No. Don't do that. She's okay."

"I talked to her and fed her breakfast. She seemed confused. Maybe this is a bad day for her. She didn't know what butter was and didn't use a fork." *He's going to fire me. But if she dies, I'd never forgive myself. I won't tolerate neglect.*

River sagged into the doorway as tension left him. A sad smile touched his perfect lips. "I appreciate how you're willing to look out for Aerwyna. She has an amazing heart. I promise you I'd never let her hurt herself. Her aide is out on the beach. There's a lot about her you wouldn't understand. Her helper has been instructed to stay out of sight unless there's an emergency. It's a very long story for another time. Just go back to work, and know Aerwyna comes and goes but she's always well protected."

Daisy pressed her lips together to hide her frown. She did her best to keep her expression neutral.

Nodding she stepped back, and he closed the door. *What a jerk. He should have told me about his sister.* Trying to push her foul mood aside, she went to the window and looked out. She couldn't see any trace of Aerwyna. Stifling her worry, she put the condiments away before cleaning off the table and bringing the dirty dishes to the dishwasher. As she got back to work all she could do was wonder about Aerwyna and why on Earth her doctors had approved such an odd form of therapy.

* * *

Daisy got the kitchen clean and sparkling. She wanted to show her new bosses she had initiative. If she only did the things on the list each day, the place would always appear half done. She pondered what to work on next as she surveyed her handiwork and enjoyed the lemony scent. Since the den was specifically off limits later, she picked up the broom and mop before heading in that direction now. Staying busy would also keep her mind off Aerwyna.

The sealed hardwood floor in the den, like the rest of the house, appeared perfect. A large decorative carpet in the great room and the sitting area upstairs were the only places she'd need the vacuum. This mop and broom were going to get to know her pretty well.

The den appeared small and messy. She could tell the guys spent time here. It smelled like them, sea breeze and something a little musky. Maybe sandalwood? Personal touches sat everywhere. She walked over to a huge bookcase. The beautiful item and carving reminded her of the railing she'd admired. Ocean had talent. She couldn't resist touching the piece. Her hand warmed under the wood, and she closed her eyes, sighing. She'd never been so comforted by furniture before. The man was a master craftsman.

When she came back to reality, she studied the different items mixed in with the books. There were shells and large pieces of polished sea glass, but also old things, artifacts. It must be amazing to own so much history. She barely knew them, yet everything in the room fit them. She could almost guess which guy had procured which item.

Unable to help herself she ran her fingers over a shelf and let the wonderful tingle run through her hand again. Her vision blurred and then her focus narrowed to a pinpoint as darkness took her. Heat rushed through her from head to toe before chills shuddered down her spine. And she was suddenly somewhere else but… not. Her mind struggled to make sense of the images that hit her as suddenly as a wave breaking on the shore.

* * *

Ocean smoothed the flyaway strands of hair off her face, and his adoring eyes flashed with his own special combination of dark jealousy and lust before he moved to claim her lips. Daisy kissed him back. She knew his lips -- his taste -- but shouldn't have. And she wanted him in the way she would a cherished lover instead of a near stranger and employer. She turned her head and leaned forward to press her mouth against his.

He groaned in response and the sound was low and feral, deep in the back of his throat. His mouth consumed hers with a delicious need that left her shaking in his arms. The delicate ache in her womb exploded to tighten her pussy and leave her gasping with momentary agony. Her wicked body demanded they fuck right now. She wanted him to let go of his controlled lust and have her with the savage passion she'd missed. Somehow in this moment she knew they'd been apart too long even though her rational mind was screaming with confusion.

Daisy tore her mouth off Ocean's and gazed into his beautiful eyes, looking for any sign he wanted her as much as she wanted him. "I need you," she confessed.

Ocean pushed her shirt up. He took a long look and grinned before playing with her breasts. "I've missed you too." He kissed each of her nipples before drawing one into his mouth with a hard pull.

Gasping, she tangled her fingers in his hair. "Never leave again. Never!"

He chuckled and she felt the rumble through her breast. The sensation only increased her pleasure. He pulled back and let go with a loud *pop*.

"Forgive me. If I could have said no, I would have." A sadness crept into his expression. "I felt every moment of your longing."

"As I did yours." Daisy wiped a drop of moisture from her cheek. She hadn't even realized she'd teared up.

"Let me make it up to you." His voice was a husky whisper. "Strip."

She didn't hesitate. He watched her. When she was naked, he walked around her in a circle looking at every inch of her. His gaze was pure love and his sense of longing pressed into her psyche.

"Lay down for me and spread your legs," he ordered.

She dropped to the soft carpet and complied. She spread her legs wide and watched him looking at her as he stripped of his clothing.

Ocean knelt between her legs. He ran his finger over her slick pussy and rubbed her clit before sticking two fingers inside of her, finding her G-spot. His thumb rubbed her clit as he found a rhythm.

Daisy closed her eyes, moaned, and shattered. She bucked. Her keening release echoed in the room as her pussy convulsed around Ocean's fingers.

"Hello," Ocean whispered soft and warm, seeming to come from much further away than she thought possible.

* * *

Daisy gasped, pulled back to reality. A bizarre sense of familiarity lingered as her eyes meet his. Heat rushed into her cheeks. She pulled herself together and pushed the vision from her thoughts as she cleared her throat. "This is beautiful."

"Thank you."

There was an awkward pause. Daisy coughed delicately because her throat was suddenly dry. "I'm -- I'm going to do my best to keep it dust free." How could she explain herself for caressing their furniture? He'd think she was nuts -- if he didn't already.

"I'm sure you will." Ocean looked at her as if seeing inside of her. She bristled a bit under his scrutiny. He wasn't as warm as River or as cold as Bayou. She couldn't put her finger on it, but she felt like he didn't trust her.

"I wasn't stealing anything." She wanted to kick herself for the defensiveness in her voice. Growing up, accused of stealing at every foster home she'd ever lived in, she never took anything from anyone.

Ocean held a book. He walked over to her. "I was just putting this back." Instead of placing it on the shelf, he took her hand off the bookcase and turned her arm, so her palm pointed up in the air. He put the book in her open hand while he held the back of her hand in his other. He gave it a gentle squeeze and peered deeply into her eyes.

Daisy hadn't realized she held her breath until she sucked in a gulp of air. His fingers were so warm. His touch reminded her of how she felt touching the bookcase, only more intense.

Ocean's brow furrowed. He let her go and stepped back. "I promise I don't think you're a thief. This is a special item. Look and touch all you like. Thank you for coming to work for us. I --" He paused as if searching for the right words. "I'm honestly looking forward to getting to know you better." He turned and left.

Daisy's throat tightened painfully, but she didn't know why. His touch had felt -- she fought to find the right description in her head -- accepting. Her eyes filled with tears, and she had to sit down for a second before shaking off the emotional overload and getting back to work.

Chapter Five

Bayou feeling pissed was nothing new. Because of the human, he couldn't let it out. If she heard the inhuman sound of his frustration there'd be no explaining it. If he destroyed things, she'd run screaming in fear.

He should scare her. He should make her run. One mistaken brush of his hand and she would never be the same again. She appeared gentle, and maybe even sweet. Anyone with those qualities should stay far away from him. Aerwyna could barely stand to look at him, and she was the kindest female he'd ever met. What would the little maid do if she learned he'd destroyed men's minds with only the stroke of his thumb? He hated how she looked at him -- like he wasn't the most dangerous thing on the island.

She was pretty. Cute, really. Daisy had a pixie-like face. The dusting of freckles on her nose only added to her aura of innocence. The darker part of him thought about what it would be like to corrupt that sweetness. Would she writhe with passion in his arms? If he could touch her, really touch her, would she come for him?

Bayou closed his eyes and tried to imagine what she looked like naked. Would that dusting of freckles also grace her chest, her abdomen? Would he be able to lay with her in bed and trace those little marks in a pattern as she chuckled with the tickle of his light touch? His gift was a curse beyond what he could endure somedays. Being alone. Being unable to feel another's body was so isolating.

The Triad had saved him from total loneliness,

but he wasn't like Ocean and River who were as attracted to men as they were women. He'd always dreamed of holding a woman in his arms that his touch didn't destroy. That constant longing would have made it easy to end his existence, but he wouldn't hurt River or Ocean by giving in to his darkest thoughts. They were the only thing that kept him anchored to life.

What would it be like to wake up with someone like Daisy? To hold someone soft and willing and loving? In his whole life he'd never had a moment of real peace. Would that morning be his first real day of happiness? The idea of loving and being loved by a woman was the only thing he wanted. He hated Daisy for being what he wanted. She was what he'd call his type. She was also kind and slightly submissive in a way that made him hard. Every time she was in the room, he was painfully erect. He knew the others knew how much he wanted her. And he felt their sympathy. The worst part? He sensed she'd have let him touch her, even given the mortal danger, out of compassion. He needed to stay far away from her.

Bayou punched the wall in the workshop. His fist left a dent in the drywall. Ocean wasn't going to be happy. That thought stole some of Bayou's rage. *Triad.* His bond with River and Ocean made them immune to him. He could choose to use *gift* on one of them, but he'd die first.

They told humans they were cousins to make the living situation less strange, but in truth they had no familial ties. Only the bond of a life vow they'd made to River. A vow had kept them from execution. A vow had saved him from the endless hell the Aegeans had put him in.

He'd come in here looking for the barometer. It

sat where Ocean said he'd left it, on the workbench, and he'd clearly worked his magic on the old piece. Bayou had a thing for barometers. They reminded him of storms. He was a storm.

Picking up the repaired item, he found a nail and hammer too. This would be perfect in the den. He knew just the spot to hang it. Most of his collection stayed in his room, but this one was special. He'd reclaimed it from the water on a recent dive, and it had called to him. Somehow, he sensed he'd needed it, but he didn't know why.

* * *

Daisy found spots for the out-of-place items in the den. She didn't want to move stuff where her new bosses wouldn't find it, but she also didn't want to leave the room cluttered. Organizing wasn't her thing. She spent more time than she'd anticipated trying to predict where they'd look for stuff.

A gruff sound startled her, and she turned. Bayou stood in the doorway. He stood stiffly, wearing a scowl and holding a barometer. Daisy smiled. Memories of the man she'd called Gramps flooded her. "That's a beautiful piece."

Bayou's eyes widened a bit. "You know what this is?"

"When I was ten or eleven, they placed me for a short stay in a foster home with an older couple. Gramps was a sailor in his youth and loved to talk. He had a similar one. Did Ocean carve it?" Daisy let the warmth of those happy days wash through her. "He was the sweetest old man on the planet. That's the only time I cried, when they moved me. He was sure I'd grow up and be a sailor just like him. I almost joined the Navy, but then I realized I wasn't disciplined enough for the military."

Bayou grunted. He remained in the doorway.

"I'm almost done here. I finished the floors and tidied up a bit. I hope you don't mind."

"Do what you want," he replied gruffly.

"Thanks," Daisy said softly. "I -- I'm sorry I make you uncomfortable."

"Who the hell told you?" Bayou glared.

"No one, um, it's just kind of obvious." Daisy would have fled but Bayou's big body was blocking the only exit.

He grunted again.

"You're not much of a talker." Daisy looked away as her cheeks heated. "I talk too much when I'm nervous."

"So, I make you nervous?" He crossed his arms over his chest.

"Um --" Daisy met his gaze. "Yeah. But it's not your fault. Sorry."

He didn't respond. When she mustered the courage to say something he gave her a small half smile, stealing her words.

"Don't worry. I have that effect on everyone." Now he looked away.

It must be hard to feel like that. Getting an idea of why he seemed aloof made Daisy glad she'd had the chance to talk to him a little. "Well, starting right now, I promise not to be nervous around you. Friends?"

Bayou glanced up at her. His eyes widened before they narrowed. "Never."

"Sorry," she said softly. "I'm trying too hard. I'm happy to have this job."

He grunted again.

"I'll just get out of your way." She picked up her cleaning supplies. "It's okay."

His expression morphed into utter confusion.

"I mean, I understand why you wouldn't want to be friends with your employee."

He muttered something about landers, which confused her. "If you could just move out of the door I'll go on to my next room."

He stepped aside. When she made her way out, he pressed against the wall as if she had a disease. She tried not to be offended. "Have a nice day. Lunch will be done at noon." She had no idea what she'd make for them to eat.

* * *

River looked around the room. No sign of Daisy. They stood in the kitchen during late afternoon. Lunch had been an interesting combination of pasta, meat, and cheese. The food hadn't killed them, but that was the best compliment he could give it. It also wasn't the light meal they'd requested. But even if she couldn't cook, he knew he hadn't made a mistake choosing her. He turned to Bayou and Ocean, grinning. "Guess who Daisy met today?"

"Did she leave the island?" Ocean frowned. He bit into another sheet of nori. None of them had eaten much of Daisy's cooking. They were standing around the kitchen island having a snack.

"Nope. Aerwyna."

"I told you bringing a human here was a stupid idea," Bayou grumbled. "What do we do now that she knows? I thought it would take at least forty-eight hours until she discovered our secrets."

"The best part," River said. "She's so kindhearted she automatically assumed Aerwyna had brain trauma and needed a caregiver."

Ocean burst out laughing, but quickly stopped and looked at the doorway to make sure Daisy wasn't coming. "She's busy, right? Are you saying she actually talked to the princess and had no clue she wasn't human?"

"I believe so, and exactly," River answered both questions. "She knows Aerwyna is my sister. I managed to convince her everything is fine, and my poor addled sis comes and goes and has a mysterious caregiver lurking around to make sure she's safe but not intrusive."

Ocean slapped River on the back. "I'm impressed. You managed to explain away the princess's very inhuman ways and any royal guard she doesn't shake on her way here. Does *Daisy* have a head injury?"

"Don't overlook the power of a good heart," River scolded.

Ocean looked down at the counter of the kitchen island where they stood. "You're right." He looked up and his gaze locked with River's. "If you hadn't had such an open mind, I'd be dead."

Bayou grunted. "Both of us. But how long can we keep up appearances?"

"One of the reasons I kept her task list light was to give us more privacy. If we're mindful," River shrugged. "Maybe we can keep her working for us as long as we stay here."

"Whatever you decide," Bayou said. "You know we're with you."

Ocean nodded.

"I haven't decided yet." River hated Aerwyna sacrificing herself. He suspected she'd only made the choice to marry Kai to buy him some time to decide if he wanted to take his father's place someday. If he did take the throne, and her marriage to Kai ended the conflict, his future would be easier. His sister humbled him. But Kai was making deals and plans in his attempt to bring about the prophecy. They just needed more proof. This tenuous truce couldn't last forever. Atlantis would suffer if Kai managed to bring about the end of the landers. You couldn't destroy the land without destroying the sea.

A ringing brought their attention to Ocean. He pulled his phone out of his pocket.

"Are you tracking him?" Ocean paused, then grunted. "Good. Keep me posted." He swiped the screen and tucked the device back.

"Reynolds Security?" River asked.

"Yeah. They've got eyes on the guy meeting with Kai. You have to go talk to your father. The further this goes, the harder it'll be to stop."

River rubbed his temples. "Father hasn't listened to me so far. He thinks the prophecy is bullshit -- of course it is, but Father wasn't there. He didn't fight in the war as I did. He has no idea how far Kai's father might be willing to go. I've seen the same fanaticism in Kai's eyes. They're hungry for power and believe they can turn the Earth into one continuous body of water."

Bayou sighed. "The old legends claim they did it with Atlantis."

River scowled. "You don't actually believe that, do you?"

"Even the landers believe. Remember the guy we had on the show who was" -- Bayou made air quotes -- "an Atlantis expert?"

"Landers have as many legends as we do. Just because somehow some ancient human learned of our city doesn't mean our ancestors were once landers."

Ocean chuckled. "If they were, Aerwyna didn't take after them very much."

River gave his friend a half smile. "There. That's all the proof I need it's all bullshit."

"When we're done learning the ways of the landers" -- Bayou put his hand on River's arm in a rare show of affection --"and completely understand what Kai is doing, are we going home?"

The question was fair, but River had no answer. He liked the life they'd built. He liked the freedom he had on land. The only thing awaiting him at home was responsibility.

Daisy came around the corner and saved him from a response. She looked a little confused. "Oh, I thought you guys would be in the den. I'm about to start supper."

"The news!" Bayou said and hurried off toward the TV. Ocean quickly followed.

"Wow, you guys really like the news," Daisy said.

River gave her a small smile and shrugged. *If she only knew the truth.* He chuckled.

* * *

Daisy foraged around in the cupboard for something she might be able to make edible. The memory of Aerwyna scarfing down French toast gave her an idea. Were these guys the breakfast for dinner type? Daisy bit her lip and tapped her fingers on the cupboard door. The guys weren't thrilled with lunch. If she wanted to keep this job she had to do better. They'd asked for privacy, but a quick question shouldn't hurt. "Right, I'll just ask," she said to herself as she walked quietly down the hall. She'd wait until she heard a commercial and tapped on the door.

The den door stood closed. She heard them talking and then the familiar baritone of Marcus Maxwell, the national news guy she thought of as kind of cute, joined the others. At least they were watching the news and not porn. She grinned. Moving closer she listened for a commercial. What she heard sounded just weird.

"Dis-ast-er," Bayou parroted after Marcus.

"You never sound natural when you say it," River said. "Try again. Disaster."

"Diz-Disast-er." Bayou's inflection reminded her of Aerwyna.

"Better," Ocean encouraged. "Nat-Nation. Hey, I got it that time."

River chuckled.

Daisy decided she would just make the French toast. Maybe they were all from some distant place and it wasn't the head injury giving Aerwyna her unique cadence... Realistically, if she wanted to hide an accent, it would make sense to watch TV to learn the local accent. She had so many questions about these guys. Maybe in time they'd open up on their own or something. She backed away from the door as quietly as she could.

Returning to the kitchen she tried to stop wondering about where they were from as she gathered her ingredients. When they spoke on their TV show, and even around her, they sounded generically American. She had to respect how hard they worked to hide their origins if they were from some far-off place. Hell, her accent wasn't going anywhere, and she'd watched the news plenty of times.

Shrugging, she started mixing up eggs and tossing ingredients into the bowl. "Well, Aerwyna, I hope you're right."

"Aerwyna?" Ocean startled her.

Daisy took a step back and tripped over her own feet. "Oof!"

Ocean caught her before she fell. His body was solid but much softer than the floor.

"Um sorry," she muttered.

"What about Aerwyna? Did she come back or something?" Ocean's dark blond brow rose as he helped get her back on her feet.

"No. I -- I was talking to myself. It's a bad habit. Sorry."

"Don't keep apologizing. I'm sure we all have quirks to get used to." He ran his hand gently down her arm. His touch tingled but it felt nice, comforting."

"Thanks. I wasn't sure if you guys were down for a little breakfast for dinner. Aerwyna loved my French toast. It's what I'm making." She held her breath, hoping he wasn't going to say they hated French toast.

"I'm sure it'll be wonderful. I'm certainly happy to try new foods."

"You've never had French toast?" Daisy's eyes widened. Didn't everyone eat the easy-to-make delicacy? Or was it just poor people who couldn't cook?

"I'm sure it's unusual, but no. Yours will be my very first." When he said it, her brain turned it into something slightly sexual and made heat creep into her cheeks. She hated how easily her mind turned perfectly nice things naughty.

River came into the room, laughing. They both glanced at him.

Ocean scowled. "Later?"

"Later," River agreed.

Daisy rolled her eyes. This one-word communication thing they had going on irritated and somehow stayed cute at the same time.

"Do you guys have a radio? A little music might be fun," Daisy said.

"We'll pick one up when we go to the

mainland," River said.

Daisy fought the urge to pout. She loved music. She'd gotten so used to Spotify she never considered what would happen here without the Internet or her phone. Did they even sell radios anymore?

The skillet was hot. She started frying the bacon.

"We're having breakfast for dinner," Ocean told River. "And Daisy is going to make me a connoisseur of French toast."

"Teasing me will earn you the burnt ones." Daisy hoped she'd manage not to burn them this time. Her grin slipped. "I won't actually burn them."

"I'm sure it'll be perfect. Accept my deepest apologies." Ocean reached out and put his hand on her arm.

His touch rolled over her skin as a comfort again. Which was weird. Instead of creeped out, she sighed, leaning into his touch. Daisy chuckled. When she turned to say something sassy, they were both smiling. She quickly returned her attention to the stove. If she let herself focus on those hotties with bodies, she'd burn the house down. Why did they have to be so hot? She should have thought to have some rando fling before coming to the island of gorgeous men. How long had it been since she broke up with Brenden? Six months? Seven? She couldn't let her dry spell drown her chances for a professional relationship with her new bosses in the waters of lust. *Focus on the bacon, Daisy.*

River chuckled.

She risked a peek at him before turning around again. *Oh no! Still hot. Ugh!*

Bayou walked in. "Is it done? I'm hungry."

"Same," Daisy said. At least one of them wasn't charming *and* hot. "Almost."

She put the bacon on a plate with thick paper toweling to absorb the excess grease and wiped out the skillet. "Shit!" She rushed to the sink and ran her burned finger under cool water.

"Let me see." Ocean took her hand away from the faucet and rubbed the damaged digit with his thumb. The pain left.

"Wow," Daisy breathed.

"Better?" Ocean's beautiful blue eyes were almost gray as he investigated her face with a kind sort of sensuality.

"Yeah."

He let go of her hand. She went back to the stove and finished cooking the meal and setting the table. She put out the same syrup and fruit spread Aerwyna had liked earlier in the day. *Aerwyna*? Worry about her still bothered Daisy. What River had told her just didn't add up.

"Have a seat, guys. It's ready." She brought the bacon and French toast to the table. "Should I save some for Aerwyna?"

River scowled. "Just stop it with Aerwyna. She's fine. Leave my family situation alone." His tone sounded so gruff it caused her to take an unconscious step back.

The guys dug in and Daisy washed up the skillet and wiped down the stove and counters. She'd lost her appetite. "Did you want me to stay here and clean up when you're done or is it okay if I go to the cottage?"

Ocean glanced up in surprise. River still hadn't looked at her since he'd told her off. Bayou didn't seem the least bit bothered.

"Wouldn't you like to sit down and have a bite before you turn in?" Ocean asked. "This is good. Thank you for introducing me to French toast."

"I'm not hungry," Daisy said.

Ocean scowled at River. That only made Daisy more upset. She didn't want to cause problems.

"We can clean up. Get lost," Bayou said.

"Thanks," Daisy muttered as she left. Maybe taking this job had been a mistake. Three more days and she could get off the island of mood-swing-men.

Chapter Six

Ocean glared at Bayou. "Get lost?"

"She wanted to go. I told her to go." Bayou took another bite of French toast. "Lander food is too damn sweet."

Ocean rolled his eyes. "You're eating it, aren't you?"

"I'm hungry."

River still hadn't said anything.

"I'd have thought you'd be nicer to her." Ocean fixed his glare on River.

When River looked up, he frowned. "What was I supposed to do? If she digs deeper, she'll figure things out we don't want her to. I'd rather have her a little mad at me now than a whole lot of freaked out later."

"And what are we going to do if -- or when -- she discovers what we are?" Ocean pressed.

"Let's hope we don't have to decide." River sighed and leaned back in his chair. "I just wish she was less curious and more concerned about herself."

Bayou grunted.

"What?" Ocean said.

River glared intensely at Bayou.

"Stay out of my head," Bayou said with a dangerous softness, making Ocean curious about his thoughts.

"Seriously, what?" Ocean asked.

"That's not going to happen," River said, looking directly at Bayou. "That's not who we are, not even you."

Bayou chuckled darkly. "Sure about that?"

"Let's all agree that, whatever happens, no harm

comes to our little maid, okay?" Ocean's anxiety clawed at him. Bayou could be unpredictable.

"Whatever." Bayou took another bite.

"We just have to be careful." River picked up his fork and pushed the food around on his plate, misery etched on his soul. "I will protect our Triad without endangering the woman."

* * *

River's head throbbed. Maybe he'd been wrong about bringing a human to the island.

There was a knock on the patio door. All three of them stiffened.

"I wonder what she needs," River grumbled as he stood up and opened the door. Daisy stood in the moonlight looking up at him.

"Hi. Can we talk about today?" She fidgeted a bit, giving away her nervousness. He didn't even need to read her mind. When she looked up at him the earnestness in her expression wouldn't let him say no.

River stepped out of the way. "Come on in. Daisy is here and would like to talk to us."

"This issue concerns you, River," Daisy replied as she stood next to the table. "Your sister was sweet. Her smile made my day. Having someone with special needs around wouldn't have been a deal breaker for me. And her condition is totally protected by the NDA. Even without the signature I'd never have told a soul. Give me more credit next time."

Ocean chuckled.

Daisy shot him a dirty look.

"I'm not laughing at you," Ocean said softly. "I never thought I'd hear Aerwyna described the way you just did. Sorry."

"And where is she?" Daisy looked at River. "It's not my place to tell you guys how to run your family, but today I saw someone who's very vulnerable. As much as I want to keep this job, I can't just sit by and let abuse happen under my nose. Even if it means you fire me." Daisy held up her hands. Abject misery filled her expression before she looked away from him. "I like it here."

Guilt hit River in the stomach. He reached out, without thinking, and took Daisy's hand. "I'm sorry. Aerwyna is a very complicated issue. I swear we weren't trying to hide her or worry you."

"Where is she? Has she eaten? Is her caregiver staying here too?"

River glanced at Ocean and Bayou. "She has a yacht of her own moored close. Her caregiver stays with her there. It's part of her therapy."

"I can't pretend that's not odd." Daisy frowned.

"I know it's not what you'd expect. The whole thing is painful to talk about." River still hadn't let go of Daisy's hand. "But knowing how much you care about a stranger's wellbeing makes me glad you're here. I promise to explain it all, someday, but not tonight."

The crease in her forehead lessened but didn't completely go away. "I'll hold you to it. Is the unfinished bedroom upstairs meant for her when she's better?"

River let go of Daisy's hand and stepped back. The person who belonged in that room definitely wasn't his sister. "We had our reasons for leaving the room the way it is. You don't need to worry about cleaning it, just like ours."

"Speaking of cleaning, Aerwyna made it sound like she'd been the one keeping this place clean. Were you making her do all the work?"

Heat crept up River's neck. "Another part of her

therapy. She's always looked out for me."

Daisy nodded. "It must be hard for her. I'd hate to be in her shoes and constantly rely on others. I get it. Can I do anything to help her?"

"If there's ever a way you can, I won't hesitate to ask. I promise."

Daisy's smile was so big and genuine. River's throat tightened. She did care. Humans were so different and yet so similar to their kind.

"Thanks. If you ever ask, I won't let you down," Daisy said. "I guess it's time for bed. Good night, everyone. I'm sorry I bothered you, but I had to get that off my mind."

"You can sleep soundly with a good conscience. I promise my sister is safe." River went to the door and opened it for Daisy as she left. Just as she was halfway out, he put his hand on her shoulder. "Knowing you care, it makes you part of the family, okay?"

Her eyes brightened with unshed tears. "That's a very nice thing to say."

"I don't say things lightly."

She nodded and left.

River shut the door and turned to see both Ocean and Bayou looking at him. Ocean seemed curious, but Bayou appeared hostile. River tried to see his thoughts and couldn't because they were so chaotic. Not a great sign when it came to Bayou.

"She's human. She could never be family." Bayou turned to Ocean. "And using *gift* so freely on her has to stop."

Ocean shrugged. "I couldn't help myself, but you're right. Triad mating with her would never work. She wouldn't even have the frame of reference to know what was being asked of her. Also, not a solution to our what-if-she-finds-out problem."

River said nothing. They couldn't see her thoughts. They couldn't know what he'd discovered about her. Daisy had almost no focus on her future self which made her more open than other humans would be to Triad mating. Kind and brave, she'd seen the darkness of the world but still had light in her.

"You said she couldn't even swim. How the hell would you bring her home?" Bayou crossed his arms over his chest. "One touch from me would send her screaming back to the mainland. I'm going to put a stop to this bullshit."

Before River could say anything, Bayou headed out the door.

"This isn't good." Ocean put his hand on River's shoulder. "If I can't stop him, at least I can do damage control." Ocean stood up and followed Bayou quickly.

River felt sick when he reached out for Bayou's thoughts again. He stood up so fast he knocked his chair over. He ran out into the night. Bayou had almost caught up to Daisy. River cringed as she turned and stopped.

He could feel her thoughts, but they were confused so he couldn't make them out distinctly. A lifetime of being defensive made her instantly afraid, and even as she reminded herself she was safe she was worried about why they'd followed her out. When the moonlight caught Bayou's expression, she became more concerned about his anger and that she'd overstepped her place than about him hurting her.

Bayou's mind was just a tangle of pain.

"No!" River shouted as Bayou grabbed her arm.

River watched helplessly as Daisy tried to jerk out of Bayou's grip. And then it hit. Flashes of terrible memories played in her mind. Bayou used *gift* like a weapon. Daisy collapsed into Bayou's arms just as he and Ocean caught up to them. Bayou laid her down carefully on the ground and stepped away from her. His touch had already done enough damage.

"I didn't know," Bayou said lamely. "Her fears are memories. I -- I wish I hadn't."

"So do I," River said gruffly as he turned to Ocean. "Can you fix it?"

"I'll do my best." Ocean picked her up off the ground and stood with her limp body. "Let's get her to bed. We won't know how this turns out until she wakes up."

They hurried into the cottage and put her to bed dressed. River pulled her sandals off and left them by the front door. When he went back into her room, Ocean sat next to her on the bed running his fingers over her face. He focused a long time at her temples. River stood in stiff silence. Bayou lurked near Ocean, pacing. Twice she turned as if fighting something in her dreams.

"Is it working?" River asked.

"I don't know. It's like she's trapped in the past. If this works, she'll remember coming home and being exhausted enough to go straight to bed. Maybe there will be a trace memory of vivid nightmares, but not Bayou's touch."

River glared at Bayou. "Why did you think you had the right to attack her with *gift*?"

"I wasn't thinking. I was just mad." Bayou remained hovering near Ocean. "When I touched her, it was like I was there with her in her past. I'd expected movie monsters or snakes, but not true evil. Humans are terrible beings."

"Not all of them," River said. "Keep your fucking hands to yourself."

"Yeah, I won't ever do that to her again. I was

wrong."

"I've never seen a human react like this to *gift*." Ocean ran his fingers over her cheeks. "It's taking all of my ability to pull her back. I don't know if it'll be enough."

"Should one of us stay with her?" River asked.

Ocean shook his head. "Too risky. She'll think she had one hell of a nightmare and had to relive a lot of traumas. If one of us is here, it would be hard to explain. I think I've done all I can."

"I just wanted her to leave --" Bayou tried to explain.

"Shut up." River cut him off. "I'm not in a very forgiving mood right now. What you did was a blatant sacrilege against *gift*. You used what made you an instrument for pain and an outcast against a helpless human because you were having a temper tantrum. I've never regretted the Triad until this moment."

Both Ocean and Bayou inhaled sharply.

"Thank you for what you've done, Ocean," River said from his heart. "But I can't be in the same room with him one more second. Make sure everything looks as natural as it can for morning."

River felt them watching him go, but he didn't turn around. He could hear Bayou's regrets and shame, but he didn't offer comfort. Everything about their Triad felt unbalanced, and River needed space.

* * *

Daisy swore under her breath, running late. She'd overslept her alarm but didn't feel rested. Going to bed last night was a blur. She'd skipped a shower and threw on some fresh clothing. Arriving to the deserted house, she noticed a note on the table.

Daisy,

We have an unexpected meeting on the mainland. We

ate. Take the day off if you feel like it. We will bring home takeout for supper, and you're welcome to join us.

River

Takeout did sound good, as did a day off because she had a whopper of a headache. Strangely, relief washed over her and she smiled, glad they were gone. Maybe it was a residual feeling from all her crazy dreams, but she didn't want to be around them today.

Her task list said today consisted of dusting and tidying. If she waited to do it tomorrow, she'd also have to add other work and be in the house longer. She decided to do the job today while they were gone. She got to work.

Hours passed and, haunted by her nightmares, Daisy couldn't focus. Maybe Sally had been right, and she should get some therapy. As the morning became afternoon, she was starting to feel better. The sound of the front door opening brought on a wave of anxiety, erasing the progress she'd made. What was wrong with her? She'd been fine with them yesterday.

River peeked into the living room where she worked, pushing a long duster into the space behind a heavy cabinet and the wall to eliminate stray cobwebs. He gave her a small smile. "How was your day?"

Daisy tried to keep her legs steady as they began to shake. "Fine."

"You seem upset. Anything the matter?" River persisted. "We brought poke bowls from the mainland."

"That's okay, I'm not hungry," she lied.

River frowned. He turned to look behind him into the other room. "Ocean?"

Ocean hurried into the room past River. He approached her so fast she flinched a second before he touched her bare forearm. "Hey, how are you feeling?"

The weird anxiety melted away. She needed to talk to a therapist. This house was safe. She was fine. What had made her so freaked out? She glanced at River and the reasonless fear didn't return. She'd skipped lunch, but when her anxiety reared its ugly head, food didn't appeal to her. "I guess I could eat if the offer is still open."

"It is." River grinned. "The place looks great. Come sit with us."

She followed River and Ocean into the kitchen. When she saw Bayou, terror slammed her so hard in the stomach she stumbled.

Ocean put his arm around her. "You okay?" He steadied her.

She glanced at Bayou. Her heart raced. An echo of fear surfaced. "I -- I'm not sure."

"Probably didn't eat," Bayou muttered. "Have some food."

She didn't want to be in the same room with him. This was too weird. Maybe he'd been in her nightmares. It wasn't fair to fear someone for something other people had done to her. "Yeah, sure, probably what's wrong with me. I just got a little --" She struggled for a believable lie. "Dizzy."

"A lot of fresh air and sun will do that as fast as too much work in a big house," River said.

Daisy panicked. "No," she said, afraid they'd think she couldn't handle the job. "Not too much work. I just got lost in it today. I promise this won't be a problem."

River scowled. "We aren't heartless jerks who would terminate you for hard work."

"Thanks," she said softly. "I -- I just felt off. You know what I mean?" But would he? She didn't even know how to explain it.

"I do. Everyone has an off day here or there. You're welcome here and we're happy to have you working for us. Settled. Let's dig in. This is from our favorite restaurant. Everything is sourced locally, and the chef's spice blend makes this the best poke you'll ever eat."

Daisy had never been a picky eater. She'd gone without enough to value a full belly. "Great. I can't wait to try it." She took the chair furthest from Bayou. He glanced at her a second before looking away with a scowl.

Ocean reached over and put his hand over hers. That bizarre sense of wellbeing surfaced again. She turned her hand over and squeezed his fingers. His touch felt just so nice she didn't even realize she was holding his hand until she noticed both River and Bayou staring.

Daisy quickly let him go and tucked the offending hand in her lap under the table. "How'd your trip back to civilization go?" She ignored the heat creeping up her neck to warm her face.

"Productive," River said. "And I hope your day was good. I can see you didn't take the offer of a day off."

"Nah, I wanted to get things done. I actually finished up a lot of tomorrow's work, too."

"Would you like to go fishing with me in the morning?" River asked unexpectedly.

"I've never been. I'm sure I'd be terrible at it." Daisy knew her flush brightened because it burned. She'd been weak-in-the-knees terrified of him a few minutes ago, but suddenly the idea of going fishing with him sounded fun. *I can't mix business with pleasure. What if I develop a ridiculous crush on one of them? I need this job.*

"I'm only asking for selfish reasons. I'd love some company out on the water, and there's nothing improper about a little fishing trip." River handed out food and wasn't looking at her.

Daisy noticed both Bayou and Ocean scowling at River. "Maybe one of your cousins would like to go? I'd hate to take someone's spot."

Ocean laughed. "I hate fishing with him. He's too competitive."

Daisy glanced reluctantly at Bayou for his reaction. He still wore a dark scowl.

Bayou looked in her direction and flinched.

Daisy flinched at the same moment.

Bayou looked away. He almost seemed... sad. "You should go. A bit of sun might do you good if you're not feeling well."

"I could finish up a few things after we eat. Did you want me to make breakfast early tomorrow?" She'd always heard fishing was a crack of dawn kind of thing.

"These two can fend for themselves for breakfast. We can eat on the boat."

"Oh, are we taking the big boat you brought me here on?"

River shook his head before handing her a poke bowl. "Nope, but our fishing boat has her share of amenities."

"How many boats do you guys have?" Daisy hoped the question wasn't rude.

"Four and the one Ocean is building," River said.

Daisy took the fork Ocean offered her. When her fingers brushed his she felt a wonderful comforting tingle. She couldn't help smiling. "You build boats too?"

Ocean shrugged. "I like to feel what wood wants

to become. It's just a hobby."

"Impressive." The heat in her cheeks rekindled. "I -- I'm a little envious. I don't have any talents." *Unless you count burning food.*

River laughed.

They all looked at him.

"Sorry." He hid his smile behind his napkin. "I just remembered something funny."

"You sure laugh a lot about nothing," Daisy grumbled.

"Maybe you just make me light-hearted," River replied.

Daisy stiffened. *Is he flirting with me? Nah, he's famous and hot. I doubt he has some pervy maid fixation. If he did, I'd be wearing a cosplay skirt only covering half my ass and one of those weird hat things. Is that a mobcap? It's going to bug me now. Yeah, mobcap, but probably the ruffly headband kind like some porn-esque anime. Oh, and totally impractical fishnet stockings. Like who-the-heck would actually get any work done? Gosh, I wish my brain hadn't taken this bunny trail.*

River cleared his throat. "So, fishing?" He put all his attention into eating his supper.

Daisy took a bite and chewed thoroughly to give herself time. *Maybe fishing will be my new thing? I could use a hobby and we are on an island.* "Sure, what time?"

River's early amusement seemed to have evaporated. Maybe she'd been too hard on him for his easy-going chuckles.

"Six, if it's not too early for you?" River still focused on his food like it might get away if he didn't look at it. *The fish must really be fresh.*

River made a noise somewhere between a cough and a laugh as he covered his mouth with his napkin.

"Six will be okay as long as you promise to make

the coffee. Are you okay?"

River flushed. "Um, yeah. Spicy bite there."

Daisy glanced down at her bowl. It appeared to be the same thing River ate and hers wasn't too spicy. *Good lord, it's good he's pretty. Wowza, he's being strange tonight.*

River put down his napkin and his lips twitched like he tried to stop a grin. "I'll make the coffee."

"I'll bring the lack of knowledge and skill," Daisy promised.

River smiled for real now. "You'll have me for a teacher. By noon you'll have caught more fish than Ocean has in his life."

Ocean snorted. "As long as you don't teach her how to gloat about her catch, she'll do great."

Daisy chuckled. "Is it competitive around here?"

"Worse," Bayou chimed in softly.

Daisy jumped. She'd almost forgotten about him.

Ocean put his hand over hers. She melted into the comfort of his touch. *That guy should be a masseuse. He'd have ladies lined up around the block for just a touch.*

A crease grew deep on River's brow. He looked down at Ocean's hand and his eyes narrowed a bit. Ocean dropped his hand. Daisy wished he hadn't.

Bayou stood up. "I'm going to bed." His tone was grouchy, and he glowered at all of them.

Daisy shrank back under his angry gaze.

Ocean reached up and brushed her cheek and chin with his thumb, cradling her face almost tenderly. Her eyes widened under his even more intensely comforting touch.

"Sorry," he muttered. "You had a little --"

Daisy grabbed her napkin quickly and wiped at her face. "Um, thanks."

"Anytime," Ocean said the word with such

extreme compassion it was almost confusing.

"Okay?" She had no idea how to respond. Her appetite fled. "I think I'll turn in too. We've got to get up earlier than those fish."

River smiled, but the expression didn't reach his eyes like it usually did. "We do. I promise it'll be fun."

"Goodnight." She picked up her leftovers to store in the cottage's refrigerator for a snack later and tossed her trash. She didn't look back when she left, afraid things might get weirder. *As if it could! These guys are just making my brain turn to Jell-O. Yellow Jell-O. The worst of the Jell-O's, yuck.*

She ignored River's chuckle as she fled.

Chapter Seven

When he was sure she'd gone, Ocean put his hand on River's arm. "Are you sure this fishing expedition is a good idea? I like her, more than I thought I would. I've seen experienced warriors do worse coming back from Bayou. He didn't hold back. I know his *gift* better than anyone else. We were imprisoned for so long it changed us. He'd torture them and I'd have to pull them back. Again and again and again --"

River put his hand over Ocean's. "Don't relive it. Are you telling me when Bayou attacked her, he unleashed full use of *gift* on her?"

Ocean could only nod. He'd seen Bayou's eyes when he'd gone after her. He'd felt the lash of angry power when Bayou touched her. The years of being forced to desecrate *gift* in such a dark way had damaged Bayou deeply. Ocean couldn't even imagine how much, and he'd been tormented the same way. Only for him, *gift* still had some purity because he'd been the one bringing those demented minds back. For Bayou it had been nothing but the bleakness. "She's strong. Bayou feels like hell about what he did."

"I know. His mind has done nothing but cry out, but I'm still mad. Maybe madder than I ever thought I could be with him."

Ocean shrugged. "I know. I'm just overwhelmed by her ability to come back out of it with only an echo of fear. She's remarkable."

"Do I need to say I told you so?" River grinned. "And she's so funny. I have got to watch myself better. She just thinks the craziest things, but they're... kind of perfect. If this maid business doesn't work out, she should try standup comedy."

"You're making me jealous I'm not the mind reader." Ocean wasn't lying.

"When you touch her and she melts for you, do you think I'm not a bit jealous?" River frowned.

"She melts, huh?" Ocean wiggled his eyebrows. "I'd be touching her a lot more if she was some other human. But seriously, I don't want her to be just a conquest. She's too -- real, you know?"

"I do," River said, and the words had a heaviness to them darkening his expression. "She feels right."

"If she is the one meant for our Triad, how will we know?"

River smiled, sadly. "Isn't it obvious?"

Ocean shook his head.

"We already do." River stood. "Good night, I'm going to bed too."

Ocean sat for a long time, alone, wondering.

* * *

Daisy gazed into the dawn. Beautiful fire lit the sky as she stood on the deck of *Aerwyna*. She grinned. River named a boat after his sister. Cute.

"Where's your sister's yacht moored?" She stood staring at the sunrise.

"The other side of the island. We won't disturb her. We'll be going out in the other direction."

"Oh, that's good." *I guess.* Daisy still worried bit about Aerwyna. She hoped she'd see her soon to verify her condition.

"Don't worry about her. She's just fine. I get a check in call regularly."

Daisy shrugged. *I have to stop borrowing trouble. My loan will come due if I keep it up.* She glanced over at River, who stood at the helm.

"Hang on, we'll be picking up speed soon."

Daisy took a seat and kept her hand tightly on the railing as chilly morning air whipped her hair around her face.

"You can go below if you'd like. I have the heater on and there's plenty of coffee."

"I'm okay," she said. "I want to see the sun rising over the ocean. It's kissing the water with flames." She felt her face heat despite the chill. "Sorry, that's a little over the top."

"It's nice. And get as 'over the top' as you like around me. Too many people out there don't say what they think."

"It's a good thing I don't. You'd be begging me to filter it if you only knew how my mind works." She laughed.

River chuckled. "I can imagine."

"When I first met you, I thought you were a mind reader." Daisy grinned. "See how twisted my head is?"

River kept the boat steady. "And if I could read your mind, how would you feel?"

"Probably traumatized. There's a reason we don't say everything we think."

"Some people say the opposite of what they think. I don't have to be a mind reader to know that's not who you are." River looked out into the ocean facing away from her.

"Yep, you're definitely not a mind reader. I don't say half of the crazy things going through my mind."

River chuckled. "If you were a mind reader, what do you think I'd be thinking about?"

"Right now, fish. A big, delicious fish fry," Daisy lied. *He's flirting with me. Even I'm able to see it and I'm flirt-dysfunctional -- zero natural flirting detection or ability. He'd probably be thinking about his maid fetish and how I should be in that cosplay outfit instead of this sweatshirt and jeans. Yep, he wants me -- I wish. Nah, I'm imagining it.* "Or a fish fry and a beer. Isn't that what all guys think about?"

"Something like that," River said stiffly.

Daisy wondered what had stolen his carefree mood. She focused on the natural glory of morning and hoped he'd return to his maybe flirting again.

As he drove something caught Daisy's eye. She squinted against the new-day sun. "River! Stop!"

The boat slowed.

"What is it?" He didn't leave the wheel but turned to look at her.

"Is a person out there?" Daisy stood up and leaned on the railing for a closer look.

"Sit down," River ordered.

Daisy did, but she tried to see exactly what bobbed in the water.

"We're heading back."

"But we haven't done any fishing yet," she protested.

River glanced at her. "Hang on." He turned the boat sharply toward shore.

Daisy sighed. She'd wanted to enjoy the day getting to know River better. Whatever had been in the water must have worried him. He knew these waters, so she resigned herself to trusting his judgment.

* * *

Pissed, River clenched his fist. Mer sight was superior to humans', so Daisy couldn't have seen exactly what he saw. He needed to get Bayou and Ocean and get back out on the water without making Daisy suspicious. The entire way to shore he considered his best option. When they docked, Daisy's frown remained. She wasn't dumb. He'd seen her thoughts pondering what had caused the abrupt change of plans.

"Daisy, could you do me a huge favor? I'm a bit worried about a wreck site close to shore we're trying to get permission from the state to survey. Could you run back to the house and tell the guys I need them? I'm sorry our plans were delayed. This is a raincheck, I promise."

Her eyes widened a bit. "What was out there?"

"I'm going to check it out with the dive boat. Tell the guys to meet me there. Hurry if you can."

She nodded solemnly. As she knew next to nothing about what he did, mind reading came in handy. She completely believed him. That fact didn't make him feel great about himself. She hurried off the boat and rushed toward the house.

Bayou arrived in less than fifteen minutes, followed closely by Ocean. He could see Daisy going in the direction of her cottage. At least that was one complication out of the way.

"When she came in with that load of bullshit, I knew it had to be a mer thing," Bayou said. "Aerwyna?"

"I wish. Kai is out there." River ran his hand through his hair.

"Kai?" Both Ocean and Bayou asked simultaneously.

"Yeah, that bastard. He wasn't alone."

"What the fuck are they doing in our waters? If we catch them breaking the truce, we have a way to get Aerwyna out of the commitment she made." Ocean grinned.

"I'm worried about why they're here. Aegeans don't like to be this close to humans and there's nothing but coastal towns all down this stretch."

"Coastal towns and us," Bayou grumbled.

"Let's get out there." River headed toward the boat they used for their diving. He wanted the boat with weapons. He'd taken Daisy out on the only craft they had that wasn't a floating armada. Most humans would never realize some of the stuff that they considered weapons. Sonic noise affected the mer nervous system fatally. They checked the boat over in record time before starting her up and piloting toward open water. If he'd been alone, he'd have confronted them with or without an arsenal. But he hadn't wanted to put Daisy in any danger just as much as he hadn't wanted her to discover their secret.

* * *

Daisy hadn't given much thought to what she'd do on a day off. She hadn't expected one so soon. The most sacred thing she'd taken to her little cottage from the main house's supplies, with her new employer's blessings of course, were coffee and filters. She hadn't tried the little coffee pot in the cottage yet. With all the drama she hadn't had a chance to let caffeine work its magic today. She glanced at the side table by the couch, spying her novel. She hadn't even gotten to the good parts of the sexy pirate tale. Today would be a nice day to get some fresh air in her lungs while reading. Consume a little coffee and she could call this multitasking.

She started to hum without even thinking about it. She'd have to thank Sally the first chance she got. It was weird not being able to send her a Snap or a text. Weird but peaceful. Without the constant distraction of social media, she began to get to know herself better. She'd spent too many years just surviving the day. Maybe the time to figure out how she wanted to survive the next year, or even five years, had arrived.

After pouring a cup of coffee when it finished brewing, she grabbed her book. Mornings were just starting to turn a little cold, so she grabbed a throw blanket she'd found in the cottage, just in case. There were a couple of chairs down by the water and she doubted anyone would care if she sat down there. This was just what she needed.

The sun had burned away the pretty sunrise, but the time remained relatively early. She sat and closed her eyes. Birds cried in the trees and the waves lapped at the edge of the island. Brisk salt air and soft breezes brushed her skin and hair like a lover's caress. She let out a sigh and opened her eyes before opening her book.

"Time to read about lover's caresses since that's as close as I'm getting to one anytime soon," she said out loud to herself as she found the page.

"We could change that. Why look at words when you could feel?" The male voice startled her so badly she spilled her coffee and dropped her book.

Daisy stood up and looked around. She didn't recognize the speaker. It definitely wasn't one of the guys.

A naked man stood up to his knees in the ocean where the tree line met the water about ten feet away. He appeared disturbingly handsome even with a scar running from his temple to his lip. Daisy glanced around for his boat but didn't see one. "What happened to your clothes?" She realized a question about what he was doing there would have made more sense, but her brain wasn't working at the moment.

"Lander, clothing is such a prudish concept. Don't you think?"

Lander? Aerwyna had used the word. "Do you

know Aerwyna? Are you her caregiver?"

He laughed as he waded out of the water and onto land. Daisy glared at him.

"Yes," agreed the nude stranger. "I will be responsible for her care, soon, but today I would see to your needs. If they are keeping you as a pet, you must be an interesting lander."

Geesh, does this guy have a head injury too? "I'm no one's pet. If you aren't currently employed as Aerwyna's caregiver, you're trespassing." Daisy tried to put as much authority in her voice as she could. "And put on your pants!"

"I do not own pants, squeamish Lander." His grin turned menacing. "I would like to know why they are keeping you."

"I don't have to tell you a thing, creep! What are you doing here?"

"It seems we are both very curious about each other. Why don't you take off your silly vestments and we can get to know what makes the other *interesting*?" He took a step toward her.

Daisy stumbled back a few paces. "Don't come any closer! I don't want anything to do with your *interesting* parts." Without any idea when the guys would be back, she started to consider her best escape route. If she went to the main house there were a lot of doors and windows which probably weren't locked. If she went to her cottage, and he got inside, would the guys hear her screams?

With no way to call for help and nowhere to run she took another step back. "How did you get here?" If she could just keep him talking until the guys returned, she might have a chance. Three fit men against one naked guy seemed like better odds than her tiny ass fighting him off. He was muscular, especially his arms.

She'd never get away if he caught her.

* * *

"Bayou! Do it!" Ocean shouted.

River struggled, pinned on his back. Kai's man had him down and tried to shove the spear he'd wrestled away into the prince's throat. As much as he hated it, they needed *gift*.

Bayou put his hand on the attacker's back.

The man let go of the spear and spun around with a wild, wide-eyed gaze.

Ocean had seen the terror many times, but it still affected him. His *gift* twined with empathy and made watching Bayou work exceptionally painful for him. Instead of calming the interloper's inner demons, Ocean grabbed the fallen spear. Another of Kai's assassins already fought the prince. River could hold his own hand-to-hand, so Ocean dispatched the one held in the grip of Bayou's *gift*. The man died without a struggle as the weapon pierced his heart. Kai's legionnaire called out a female name as he died experiencing his greatest fears. Ocean's soul weighed heavy, but right now he couldn't focus on the darkness.

Bayou headed toward the one fighting River.

"Don't!" Ocean called. "Not unless you have to." His concern reared up for Bayou's mental state more than for the enemy. Every time Bayou used *gift* it made the light in his soul fade a little more. Someday he'd be beyond Ocean's ability to heal.

As they approached, the one River had fought dove off the side of the boat. As he hit the water, they saw the flick of his tail as he took his truest form. The bastard was fast, but Ocean found the fallen modified hydrophone. This wasn't for listening; it created a sound only mer-kind could hear. As Ocean hoisted it over the side of the boat Bayou watched to make sure it submerged.

Bayou looked back to River and nodded. "Now."

River threw the switch connected to the boat's battery. Even on the boat they suffered from the screech but underwater, they'd be paralyzed by it. Five minutes of the sound in the ocean and they'd die, unable to filter oxygen through their gills. They didn't use this weapon lightly. But protecting the prince was the most important thing. Leaving even one assassin to lurk near the shore was unacceptable. Raised as enforcers in Kai's father's palace, the men would kill without remorse. Neither intruder had demonstrated a very powerful use of *gift*.

"These were dispensable." Ocean glanced at Bayou who watched the timer.

River ran his hand through his hair, scowling. "And Kai never boarded. We need to get back to shore. Something isn't right. I think we were lured out here."

"Shit," Bayou muttered. "What if Aerwyna backed out of the commitment? This is the first place she'd come."

"How long on the timer?" River's jaw clenched.

"Just over three minutes." Bayou watched the timer as if he were willing it to move faster.

* * *

Daisy took another step back. She had to keep Naked McCreepy talking.

"I swam, of course." Naked guy chuckled. "You are not smart."

Her eyes narrowed. "At least I have pants!" She bit back her comment about the cold and his shriveled junk. She only wanted to keep him talking, not anger him into attacking.

"Unfortunately," he said, dryly. "Would you like

to take them off now? You should be honored a sea prince would even want you."

What is up with all this prince stuff? "Well, your majesty, why have you come to grace our humble little island?"

"Ah, you jest with me. Very rude, lander. I am here for my princess." He put his hands on his hips, which only served to remind Daisy this emperor needed new clothes.

"I'm not her. I guess you'll have to swim away to another island." She waved her hand at the ocean in the universal gesture to go away.

A splash caused them both to turn toward the water. *Aerwyna.* What was she doing so far out in open water? There wasn't a boat to be seen and she seemed too far from shore. Daisy panicked. She had to protect the poor woman from this jerk. A dude showing up naked and propositioning a stranger would likely take advantage of a disabled person.

A large piece of driftwood lay a few steps away in the sand. As Daisy made a move toward the wood, she noticed a big fish's tail near Aerwyna. Her breath caught. She squinted and peered more closely at the woman. Was she wearing a costume in the water? Bizarrely the fish tail appeared to propel Aerwyna forward unnaturally fast. Naked guy turned to look out toward Aerwyna. Using the distraction to her favor Daisy made it to the wood and picked it up.

Naked guy took a couple steps in her direction but stopped as she swung the makeshift weapon.

"Stop! You're going to leave right now," Daisy ordered.

"Such a passionate lander. I would have enjoyed seeing that fire used for better things, but my princess is here now."

He turned away, completely unconcerned with Daisy, and stepped into the water.

Daisy could see Aerwyna clearly at this distance. She wore a tail! There wasn't some big fish behind her. "Look out." Daisy cupped her hands around her mouth in hopes the sound would carry farther. "There's a naked guy swimming toward you." From the corner of her eye, she saw another of the big fish tails. "What the fuck?" she gushed the question out loud. But as naked guy approached Aerwyna she didn't have time to fully grasp what she saw. He grabbed Aerwyna's beautiful hair.

Daisy ran thoughtlessly into the water. She couldn't swim, but she couldn't just stand there and watch either. Aerwyna splashed and fought. Holding her wood above the water, Daisy waded out into the freezing ocean until the water floated up to her armpits. They weren't that far off. "Over here. I'll hit him. Get over here."

Aerwyna struggled. She splashed and pulled. They were closer. Daisy took another step. The ocean floor dipped lower than she'd expected where she put her foot. A current pushed her. Panic. Nothing solid remained under her feet. She kicked and pulled at the water with her free hand. Her mouth opened as she gasped for air, and she tasted the salty water. Coughing and sputtering her foot hit something solid and Daisy struggled backward in the water until both feet were on the edge of where the ocean floor dropped. She shook, but still had hold of the driftwood.

Aerwyna's desperate gaze found Daisy's.

"Closer!" Daisy raised the wood over her head. The struggling pair were almost there.

Daisy brought the wood down across the man's

shoulders and back. She raised her arm again and this time she connected to his head like she swung a baseball bat.

He screamed something totally unrecognizable in a shrill tone that made Daisy stumble back. She almost lost her footing but managed to stay upright in the current.

When the stranger turned to her, his eyes shone with an unnatural light. Terror made Daisy want to struggle for the shore, but determination kept her fighting to help Aerwyna. In the distance she could hear a boat.

Naked guy let Aerwyna go. He turned and came at Daisy. She swung her weapon again, making contact with the side of his head, but the blow didn't stop him. His strong hands gripped her arms, and he shook her. The wet wood slipped from her fingers. She lost her only weapon to the ocean current. Her attacker shook her again and she no longer had any footing. Daisy went under. She kicked and struggled to find a handhold on the man's wet skin. She pushed up, and as her head broke the surface she screamed. Gulping in a breath she struggled with panic as he took her back under the surface. Daisy fought for her life.

* * *

River dove off the side of the boat. "Wait!" Ocean called, but he didn't stop the painful transformation of his body. The fabric ripped around his legs as his tail emerged and he pushed forward with the power of his true form. When Kai pulled Daisy under the water, the secret didn't matter anymore.

"Brother, help her," Aerwyna's voice hit his mind in the way the mer normally communicated underwater. He could see his sister trying to pull Kai away, but she wasn't strong enough to get the

powerful male to release his victim. River pushed himself harder. Bayou swam past him. River might be a strong swimmer, but Bayou and Ocean were both faster due to years of grueling battle training.

When Kai saw Bayou, his eyes widened, and he let go of Daisy. He knew all too well the power of Bayou's cursed *gift*. Daisy wasn't moving. When Bayou reached her, he hovered helplessly near her body, unable to touch her. Aerwyna made it to her first and pulled Daisy up so that her face rose above the water. River felt sick as he watched his sister swimming toward shore with the motionless human. In the distance Ocean moored the boat and rushed down onto the beach.

Aerwyna transformed closer to shore and finished her swim with legs. River joined her and together they got Daisy back on land. River checked for a pulse. Joy burst through him as he felt a heartbeat, but when he put his ear close to her mouth and nose, she wasn't breathing. He had to get the water out of her lungs. He tilted her head to open her airway. As he started CPR she coughed. He helped her turn to her side and water poured from her mouth as she kept gasping and spewing up more water.

He grabbed Aerwyna's hand as she began pounding too forcefully on Daisy's back.

"*She's human. Cease.*" He sent the thought to his sister.

"Are you living?" Aerwyna asked Daisy.

Daisy kept coughing but nodded her head. Ocean knelt beside Daisy and, as he put his hand down to touch her, River stopped him. "Let her body recover before you try to calm her mind."

They were so busy attending to Daisy that when Bayou grunted with pain River almost didn't look his way. Kai and three mer were on the beach.

Daisy pushed herself up on her arms. She lowered her head, still coughing.

"Aerwyna, you've broken your word," Kai said in the Aegean tongue.

"I saw those children! What you're doing is the darkest blasphemy. Torturing them to twist the emergence of *gift* shames your people. May the gods curse you. Even for a real chance at peace I will not tie my life force to a monster," Aerwyna replied in the same language.

River's eyes narrowed. He knew the kind of brutality Kai's empire inflicted on adults. The idea that they were manipulating *gift* in children enraged him. Maybe it was time to go home. As much as he enjoyed living among the humans, he'd learned enough to return with knowledge that could help his people.

"Get the human," Kai ordered his men.

"She has nothing to do with this." Bayou stepped between Kai's minions and Daisy. His *gift* being the most powerful of the trio made the interlopers pause. They looked to their prince.

"She has seen too much and must die." Kai stood safely back and crossed his arms over his naked chest.

One of the guards rushed them and Bayou grabbed him. A scream tore from him with agony that transcended words. But the other two kept coming. Ocean lunged for one of the men and tackled him to the ground. River noticed the men weren't used to land and he put that to his advantage as he sprang at the remaining adversary. It wasn't difficult to knock him on his ass.

He twisted under River, but as his hands came around River's throat, he took a handful of sand and tossed it into his enemy's eyes.

Daisy shrieked.

River turned, but the distraction cost him his advantage. He only caught a glimpse of Kai hauling Daisy toward the ocean. Aerwyna clutched onto one of Kai's legs, tripping him, and he fell. Daisy started to run up the beach. River fought the choking grip as the man on top of him clutched his throat.

* * *

Daisy ran. She didn't know where to go, but she wanted to get away from the water. Naked guy was going to drown her again for sure. Though her mind was fuzzy, she'd never heard the language they'd all been speaking. She knew both River and Aerwyna had tails. She had to get off this island. The boat sat moored up ahead. If she could get to it and start it, maybe she could figure out how to drive the big thing. She needed to get as far away from this crazy island as possible. Sally owed her for getting her tangled up in this mess.

A sudden, painful grip and sharp yank on her wrist forced a scream out. Pain radiated up her shoulder. Something must be dislocated.

"Do not run from me, lander." Naked guy tugged her closer. His strength was unnatural.

She grimaced and tried to push away from him, but he held her close. "Let go!" she screamed.

"It is a shame you must join the water. Your life will honor the creatures that take subsistence from your death."

Daisy slapped him across the face with her good arm, but he managed to pin it to her side as he walked her backward toward the ocean.

"Help!" she cried. No matter what kind of beings her new bosses were, they wouldn't let this freak kill her. She hoped. "He's strong!"

She buried her wet shoes in the sand and tried to

hold back as he dragged her toward the water.

"Come quietly to your death and I will be merciful." Naked guy twisted her injured arm and her knees buckled.

"Stop!" she begged as tears of agony clouded her vision.

He tugged harder, still twisting, and the world swam, narrowing into darkness. She wrestled for consciousness and lost.

Chapter Eight

River homed in on the mind of his attacker. He hated to twist *gift* like this, but there was no time to fight another way. *Release me!*

The man's mind rebelled against the order.

Release me. Return home. All you want is home. You do not want to be with the landers another second. Your skin is crawling. You need the ocean. River pushed the desire to flee into the man's subconscious.

River's opponent let go and scrambled back on his hands and heels. He rubbed his neck as he watched the mer enter the water, transform, and disappear under the waves.

Daisy! River scanned the beach for her and couldn't see her. He glanced up toward the buildings. Then he heard a splash. Turning, he saw Kai dragging her limp body below the waves.

"No!" River roared as he pushed up. Ocean still fought, and Bayou struggled. River didn't have time to pull him out of *gift*. The screams of the unfortunate in his grasp were pitiful.

Surf hit River's naked legs as he ran into the water. He gave in to his nature and a throbbing ache let him know the transformation had completed as he dove into deeper water and swam toward where he'd last seen Kai. Panic filled him as he realized Daisy wasn't moving again. He watched Kai holding her under the water and the sick joy on the other prince's face brought a darkness into River that he'd only felt on the battlefield of the coral caves.

It's too late, Kai sent thought communication. *Your lander will feed the creatures of the ocean now.*

A spark of life remained in Daisy even if her heart had stopped. His *gift* gave him the ability to feel her essence even as it ebbed.

My Triad claims her. He sent the thought without thinking of the consequences. *Let her go.*

Kai's humor tingled like a painful sensation in River's mind. *You cannot claim the dead.*

Let her go and I will prove she lives.

Kai's thoughts were a muddle of triumph and confidence that Daisy was dead. His twisted soul relished dark images of what he could do to her corpse. He let her go and she floated toward River.

River took hold of her and pulled her close. When he pressed his mouth over hers, he blew the oxygen created by his gills into her mouth and he pressed *gift* strongly. *Live, Daisy. Join us.*

Daisy's eyes opened and she struggled in confusion.

River held her close. *I've got you. I will breathe for you. Trust me.* He blew more life-sustaining air into her lungs. *My Triad claims you. We will protect you. We will cherish you. Do you consent?*

Her brow furrowed.

Nod if you consent, lander. Kai sent the communication to them.

River doubted Daisy could hear him. When she nodded, River almost lost his grip on her. She closed her mouth when he pulled away from her in surprise.

Kai scowled. *Coincidence. Lander, if you can hear me and you would tie your life force to those abominations, nod.*

Even underwater River could see the confusion on Daisy's face, but she nodded. He pulled her close again and blew more air into her mouth.

Such a worthless Triad wouldn't be fit for a mer-

female. Let the sea rot you. Tell your sister that I will not have her. There will be no peace.

As much as River wanted to catch the bastard and fight him, he had to think of Daisy. Her human body wasn't made to stay in these low temperatures for long. He could feel her shaking against him. Trauma and shock might also take her life. River breathed for her again.

The mer-male that had fought Ocean swam past them following Kai. River reached out through the bond of Triad and relief washed through him when he felt Ocean's life force endured. Kai's legionnaire held something in his hand, but River had no time to go after him.

Hold me tight." River sent the thought to Daisy. Amazingly, she heard and complied. He swam with her arms wrapped around his neck and her legs wrapped around his waist. He made sure to keep her head above water. She seemed surprisingly calm considering what had just transpired. What would Ocean and Bayou say? He'd just tied Daisy to them without their approval. If one of the others had tried, the bonding wouldn't have worked, but as alpha of the Triad his power over their lives was total. Guilt nibbled at him. She would have died without his life force. There hadn't been much left in her when he'd arrived. But now he could feel life surging through her as strongly as a mer. She connected with them and united the Triad in a new way now.

* * *

When River made it to shore, he had his legs again. Daisy still clung to him. He could feel the shock of his friends through the bond.

I had to. He sent the thought and got no response. How angry would they be? Her life was worth a little -

- or a lot -- of the others' wrath.

"Give her to me," Ocean said with tenderness in his tone. "One of them went to the house before escaping."

River would deal with that information later. He found himself reluctant to hand Daisy over, which surprised him. Ocean took her from him gently.

Aerwyna stood next to Bayou, trying to talk him into releasing the mer-male he held in the thrall of *gift*. She risked her life. He could turn on her in his all-consuming trance. River struggled, torn between going to Bayou and following Ocean. Normally, Ocean would have been able to bring Bayou back, but his attention focused on Daisy as he carried her toward the cottage. River glanced back, relieved to see Bayou pull his hands away from the man he'd held. He stumbled away from Aerwyna. Disgust etched Bayou's face. River knew this would horrify Bayou when he came back to himself over how he'd destroyed his opponent, even if the male belonged to Kai's legionnaires.

Ocean struggled to hold Daisy and open the cottage door. River rushed up and helped. They got her inside and laid her on the bed.

River stood helplessly as Ocean released *gift* fully. He pulled himself together and grabbed some towels. He stumbled mid-step as he entered the small bathroom. A strange moment prickled through him where the Triad bond seemed to encompass him. He had to lean against the bathroom vanity for a moment. The beat of life force altered. And Daisy fully joined with them. His heart thundered in his ears, and he closed his eyes. A rightness settled over him. He found what he was looking for and returned.

"Did you feel it?" Ocean's voice shaded with awe.

"Yes." River couldn't manage more than that. His throat tightened.

"Bayou?" Ocean's hands still ran over Daisy's wet arms and face.

"Aerwyna pulled him back. I think he'll be okay. His thoughts -- he's hurting."

"I know," Ocean replied. "I wish -- We have to focus on her now."

River nodded. "She feels strong."

"I've done all I can."

"It will be enough," River said with a confidence he didn't fully feel. "Let's get her wet clothing off."

"Maybe we should ask Aerwyna? I -- I don't want to make her uncomfortable. Even with what she's committed to, she might not like us stripping her."

River grunted. He went outside. Aerwyna tried to talk to Bayou, but he wasn't listening.

"Sister, come here," he shouted in his native tongue.

Aerwyna gave Bayou a final, sad glance before she hurried up to the cottage. "How did you save her? She's brave for a lander." She also spoke the language of their people.

"Triad."

Aerwyna stopped and gaped at him. "You're joking!"

"No. The bond is strong. She would have died. We would ask you to help us preserve her modesty. Let's get her into some lander nightclothing."

Chuckling, Aerwyna followed him inside. Her thoughts were clear. She thought landers prudish and wondered how Daisy would feel with three virile males in her bed.

"It may come as a shock," River replied to her thoughts.

"May? At least you have the sense to have asked me for help. She kept Kai from taking me prisoner. I have much to thank your lander for. I am pleased to help her, brother. Father will not be pleased."

"When has Father ever been pleased with my choices?"

Aerwyna went to Daisy's dresser and pulled out a T-shirt and some fluffy pants. "This should be modest and comfortable during her recovery. You've gotten her bed all wet. Pick her up and I'll do what I can to correct this."

Ocean picked Daisy up and cradled her close to him. She shivered. Her human body was so frail. Even with their combined life force, River worried she'd grow ill, or her mind wouldn't recover from the day's trauma. He tried to keep his expression neutral to prevent the others from worrying with him.

As Aerwyna made the bed, Ocean's lips twitched. "I didn't believe the princess of Atlantis knew how to make a lander bed." He spoke Atlantean, the language of his earliest youth, but from his many years conscripted against his will to the Aegeans there was an accent to his words.

"Who has been keeping filth from your dwelling?"

Ocean grinned. "I couldn't resist teasing you."

"Indeed? You are lucky I love you as an extension of my brother's soul. I respect your lander. It should be interesting seeing your Triad complete. I will also be keen to see how you three will manage this. Outside of the old tales I do not believe any mer has been foolish enough to attempt mating with a human. It's good she has courage." When she'd finished, she looked at the bed and then Daisy. "You." She pointed at Ocean. "Turn your head and hold her for me." She pointed at River. "You. Leave."

River obeyed his younger sister. A few minutes later, Aerwyna popped her head out of the bedroom. "She's modest."

River returned to see Daisy under the covers.

Ocean cleared his throat. "About what was taken… we need to search the house."

"Kai stole something?" Aerwyna asked.

"Possibly. One of them went into the house during the chaos. I saw something in one of the legionnaire's hands, but I had to get Daisy to shore."

"You made the right choice," Aerwyna said. "I can sit with her if you need to investigate."

River didn't want to leave Daisy, the bond they shared too new to leave. The idea of her waking up without them there bothered him.

"Go. She will be well looked after. She is my soul sister now. I would let nothing harm her. I am not a stranger."

River sighed. "Ocean, find Bayou. I'll investigate the house."

Ocean nodded.

River gave Daisy one final look before he left the room. This bond, different from what he felt for the others, completed him. He just hoped Daisy was up to the challenge of being mated to a mer -- *three* mer.

* * *

Ocean found Bayou sitting on a rock, staring into the water. "She's safe. River is checking the house." He spoke English just in case some random human happened to come to the island.

Bayou grunted.

"It'll work out with Daisy."

Bayou said nothing. His frown deepened.

"She's resting. I tended her with *gift*. I'm sure

she'll want to see all of us when she wakes up."

When Bayou turned, his expression twisted with torture. "I'm a fucking monster. And now that innocent human is tied to me for the rest of my life. I should end myself to save her."

"We don't know how your *gift* will react to her. You can touch me and River. Why would you think it'll be different with her?"

"Even if I can touch her, my soul is filth. She doesn't deserve this. What the hell was River thinking?"

"We haven't had a chance to discuss what happened out there, but he said she'd have died. You were consumed and likely didn't see Kai dragging her into the water. He had her under much longer than any other lander could survive."

"I felt it," Bayou said softly. "I felt the bond take hold. It was so strange. She's just kind of there with me now."

"I know." Ocean went over and sat next to Bayou. "I felt it too. It's warm, soothing."

"That's different. She feels different from you and River. I --" Bayou's voice broke. "I couldn't endure it if I got lost in *gift* and somehow touched her. If she dies you both die. We all die. And the fact that she's human and has a much lesser life span --"

"Don't," Ocean cut him off. "When River saved our lives with Triad, he knew what it was to tie our life forces together. He knew the extent of your power. We trusted him once with our lives, and now we have to do that again. With our life force in her there's a good chance her days will be extended far past that of a normal human."

"But to ask Daisy to belong to us feels wrong. She's young, and don't all humans expect to be wooed by a lover before committing?" Bayou ran his hand through his wet hair. "She -- she didn't have a choice."

"But she wouldn't have any of those things if Kai had killed her. We can make her happy." Ocean reached out.

Bayou jerked away and stood, pacing in the sand. His fists balled at his sides. "Hell, she can't even swim. She can never be fully immersed in our world. And I'm unworthy."

"What is it the humans say? Aren't we all imperfectly perfect?" Ocean reached out and took hold of Bayou's forearm. He pressed *gift* with all the hope he could muster.

Bayou pulled out of his grip. "Don't waste energy on me. You may need to tend to her again later."

"Come to the cottage. Please."

Bayou stopped pacing and let out of huff. "Sure. But when she runs screaming from me, don't tell me I didn't warn you."

River approached with palpable anger. "The seal is missing."

Ocean frowned. "The first king's seal?"

"Do I own more than one seal?" River rubbed his face. "Sorry. Yeah. Father will kill me. That one you fought must have had a finder *gift*. I'd wondered why Kai would show up here with a B team. Those were not his best legionnaires; they were far too easy to dispatch. I bet every damn one of them were finders. Damn it!"

"There's nothing we can do about it right now. Let's go check on Daisy." Ocean stood up. "And get some dry clothing."

They all walked down the beach. But this was the first time they'd been together without being complete.

The need to go to her called like a siren's song.

* * *

Daisy opened her eyes and squinted against the sunlight coming from the window. Had she overslept her alarm? She'd had the strangest dream. Awful. Mermaids -- men? She had to remember not to eat before bed. Her imagination was better than she'd thought. She started to laugh but it quickly turned into a groan. Her head throbbed with splitting agony.

"Living is good, flower lander. Pain is alive."

Daisy gasped and sat up in bed, which only made her moan and grab her head. "Aerwyna? How did you get in here? What time is it?"

"It is only small hours since we kicked Kai's ass to water. You are brave."

"Are you telling me that wasn't a nightmare? Oh my God. Your brother is a --" Daisy ignored her pain as she tried to get out of bed. "You're a --" She needed to get off this island.

"Rest now. And yes, we are mer. You belong to Triad now."

Daisy heard the door open. She shuddered. "I need to get out of here. Back to the mainland."

River walked in. His expression tightened but still managed to be neutral. "You're safe. No one is going to hurt you."

Aerwyna sagged as if relieved and sat down on a chair across the room. "Brother is kind. Talk."

"What did you do to me?" Daisy couldn't keep the accusation out of her tone.

"I saved your life." River's brows drew together. "I'm sorry about how I had to do it."

"He's good at tangling people into his life force," Ocean said lightly as he entered the room.

"What? Make some sense," Daisy ordered.

"Please, my head is killing me."

Ocean sat down next to her and she tried to scoot away, but he reached out and took her hand. "Let me help." He put his fingers on her temples. The pain ebbed. Ocean groaned. The pain subsided completely. He had to catch himself to keep from tipping over.

"You can't keep this up." River put his hand on Ocean's shoulder. "You're done."

Ocean nodded.

Daisy noticed Bayou lurking in the doorway. He'd made one of the attackers scream like she'd never heard anyone scream. "Okay, Ocean has some kind of healing mojo. River, you *have* been reading my mind, haven't you? And Bayou, you're like -- a what?"

"A killer," Bayou replied without a hint of emotion.

Note to self, don't piss him off. "Gotcha, so do I have superpowers now too? What did you do to me in the water?" She looked at River.

"I tied you to my Triad's life force." River glanced away. "Mer mate for life. Your life force and ours are united."

"And that means…" Daisy had no idea.

"It means you are part of me -- us for the rest of our lives." River frowned.

"So if you die, I die?" Daisy's eyes widened.

"The mer have a much longer life span than humans. We *will* keep you safe."

"What if I die first?" Daisy ignored his scowl.

"Then we die. You become the center of our existence."

"Like that's not pressure." Daisy rolled her eyes.

"I mean it," River said. "You'd be our entire world. We've always wanted a mate, but never expected her to be human."

"You did this to save my life. Can you undo it when you find your mate? Are you actually cousins? And your names are totally bogus, right?" Daisy flopped over onto her side and huffed. "Oh my God, I have so many questions."

River shook his head. "We aren't related in any way. Telling humans we were family made our bond more understandable. You'd never be able to say our true names, so we took English words that meant the same things. Mer don't have surnames, so we created one. There will be much for you to learn because you are our mate. Don't you feel it? This bond cannot be broken except by death."

Daisy bit her lip. "What if we get in a big fight?"

Ocean chuckled and they both paused to look at him. "I imagine we'll have our fair share. You do have three men to manage, after all. I know this is different from what you envisioned for your future too."

"Honestly." Daisy sat up. "I never gave a soulmate or whatever much thought. I -- I've never believed in forever."

Bayou grunted. "Get comfortable with it."

"Helpful," Ocean mumbled. "Ignore him. For our kind it's not the same choice as it is with humans. We won't just wake up one morning and decide it's over. Our lives and powers are tied together in the most sacred and intimate bond. Humans have nothing to compare it to. I'm sorry."

"Wow. That is seriously messed up." Daisy felt tears prickling behind her eyelids. These guys had lost their chance to find someone they wanted just to save her. "I'm *more* sorry. You lost your shot at finding the perfect woman and ended up with me." She couldn't bear to look up and see the truth of how disappointed they all must be.

Ocean ran his fingers lightly down her arm. "We aren't pining for some mer-female swimming around in the sea. You have nothing to be sorry for."

Daisy risked a glance up. River didn't seem mad or regretful. Ocean smiled at her with his gentle kindness.

Bayou was still frowning with his arms crossed over his chest, but when his gaze met hers some of the stiffness left his posture. "Could have worked out worse for us."

Daisy kept her grateful smile.

Bayou's frown deepened. "When I touch you, you won't be smiling anymore."

"Are you threatening me?" Daisy's eyes narrowed. She'd have gotten off the bed to flee if River hadn't put his hand gently on her shoulder.

"No. But let me show you." Before the others could stop him, Bayou rushed across the room and put his fingers on Daisy's temples.

"What?" Daisy asked. "What are you planning to do?"

"I -- I'm doing it?" Bayou's voice trembled. "It's not working."

"Thank gods!" Ocean pushed Bayou away. "That was shitty. What would you have done if it worked?"

Bayou shrugged. "Had to know."

"What?" Daisy asked again.

Bayou looked her straight in the face. "I kill with fear. My touch makes people experience their worst nightmare. If I do it long enough the person dies."

"You tried to kill me?" Daisy gasped.

"Not exactly. I'd have stopped right away if it'd worked, but you'd have seen the real me. I would never kill you."

"That's a relief," River said. "But what isn't is the

fact Kai stole my seal."

"Father will --" Aerwyna had stayed silent until now. She made a stabby motion in the air. "Death you!"

"I'm aware," River grumbled.

"Father will not death you if I talk to him." Aerwyna stood. "I will make him understand."

River grimaced. "As much as I'd like to wait to tell him, you're right. It has to be done."

Aerwyna crossed the room to kneel before Daisy. She touched her cheek gently. "No fear."

Daisy put her hand over Aerwyna's and shook her head. "No fear."

Aerwyna brightened as she stood up and looked at each of the three men. "You all be nice. Flower lander is not around powerful males until now. Human males are little fish."

River's brow hitched. "What human males do you have experience with, sister?"

Aerwyna chuckled. "No need for death. Movies give me excellent words. Even the prettiest movie men are little fish when mer-males are near."

"Swim safe currents, sister." River bowed his head and closed his eyes.

Aerwyna duplicated the gesture before she left.

"It's going to be awkward for you the next time you see your father," Bayou said, looking at River.

"I'm not going anywhere for a while. We have to protect our mate. There's no way I'm leaving the people who matter most to me when we don't know everything Kai is planning."

"What is the seal? Why did Kai want it? Is that why he attacked your sister? Get me up to speed here." Daisy stood up but wobbled.

All three men rushed to steady her.

"Jeez, I'm fine. Seriously, what's the deal?"

"Sit back down and I'll tell you," River replied.

Daisy sat on the mattress.

"Good." River ran his hand through his hair and gazed out the window a moment before turning his attention back to Daisy. "There's a prophecy. When the princess of Atlantis gives the great seal of the first king to the Aegean prince of her free will, the sea will become the Earth."

"That's it?" Daisy asked.

"Yep." River sighed.

"Dire." Daisy rolled her eyes. "And silly. Does the seal have some kind of magic powers?"

"It's just a golden disk. Nothing more magical than any other relic of the past." Ocean put his arm around Daisy and held her. "I'm sorry foolish belief stole your choices."

"I'm alive. I'll take three hotties with bodies over death any day of the week." She looked away so he wouldn't see the real sadness she tried to hide.

Ocean gently turned her face back and gazed into her eyes intently. "We will keep you safe. You believe that, right?"

She honestly didn't know what to believe.

Chapter Nine

Daisy jerked in surprise when Bayou touched her shoulder.

"I won't hurt you," he muttered.

"I'm not afraid of you. You startled me. I'm still overwhelmed." Daisy was glad he'd freed her from having to answer Ocean.

"Well, Kai's an idiot. He has what he wants so maybe he'll stay in his own currents." Bayou put his hand back on Daisy's shoulder gingerly. "I -- I can't believe I can touch you."

"What is this thing, anyway? River said we are bonded, and our lives are tangled together. Someone called me a mate. What does that even mean? Bayou, you won't sugarcoat it. Tell me the truth."

"It means you're the only woman that we'll ever want in our life. You're part of us in a way that's more than some legal document or a friend. We will want you until we die. Our last breaths will be agony because our death means you've gone first." He didn't look at her until he'd finished. "But that feeling inside you means we're complete now. You'll never be alone again, Daisy."

"I don't have any idea how to wrap my head around what you just said." Daisy's throat tightened.

"Humans have no frame of reference for a mating bond or Triad. Don't worry. We'll figure it out."

She was pretty sure those were the most words Bayou had said to her in their brief acquaintance. "Do you have to have a Triad?"

Bayou chuckled. "River? You want to take this

one?"

River nodded. He sat down on the chair Aerwyna had vacated earlier. "There's been war between my people and Kai's for a very long time. His people have a much darker craving to win and to see the world destroyed. They see the societies on land as a threat. Bayou and Ocean were children when the millennia-old travel systems were blocked by the Aegean legionnaires. They were enslaved and had *gift* weaponized as it emerged in them. Children don't always show signs of what they'll eventually be able to do unless they have a powerful *gift*. They were taken from their parents. The terrible things they had to do weren't by choice. During a particularly deadly battle, which led to a tenuous truce of sorts, my father's army captured both of them. To save them from execution I enacted the bond of Triad."

"Why?" Daisy couldn't help interrupting.

"Because what had been done to them was wrong and I couldn't stand by and watch another wrong happen. It's been centuries since Triad has been practiced as a regular custom. The ocean is a dangerous place. Women were scarce for our ancestors. Three men could protect their female and her children better than one. Before this war, our kind enjoyed a long stretch of peace. Triad became rare. It's hard to share the person you love and harder to entrust your life to others." River glanced at both Bayou and Ocean. "They were pretty shocked when I did it. But it did keep my father from having them killed. Your choice wasn't the first I've stolen to give someone a tomorrow."

"Okay. So where do we go from here?" Daisy focused on some sand on the carpet to avoid looking at any of the men.

"Where do you want to go?" Ocean asked softly.

"I want all of us to be happy. I don't want you guys to suffer because I didn't die." Daisy still couldn't look at them. "I've never been a girl who believed in fairytales or happily-ever-after I'm not asking you guys for that."

Ocean chuckled. "Well, you are the mate of a prince. Maybe it's time you start believing."

When Daisy looked up at him, he captured her lips with his. At first, the kiss moved slowly and sweetly. She relaxed into the sensation. Kissing him back felt like the most natural thing in the world. Being close to him felt right, but also oddly wrong. It didn't feel like cheating; more like missing a piece of him. When he pulled back to look at her, she opened her mouth to tell him and closed it again. How could she even explain?

"I know," River said. "Watching him kiss you, it felt like I held you too. It's not something you've ever experienced with a human man. When you're ready, we will be your friends, your protectors, your lovers. You are our everything."

* * *

Daisy cringed as her face heated. She couldn't make eye contact with them, not even River. "I don't expect us to always share a bed, but tonight I want you all near me. Is that okay? I'm -- I'm more comfortable doing this here."

"You want to have sex -- with us -- tonight?" Bayou asked.

River slugged him in the arm, hard. "What he means is, if you need time we understand."

"I think I do. I know it's weird, but I think I need it because of how crazy everything is right now. I just want to feel the bond. Does that make sense?" Daisy's face burned hotter.

"You don't have to explain it to us. And it's not something you should feel shame over. Our kind don't have the same hang-ups as humans do. If you'd have us all every night not one of us would protest. But even if you are only ever comfortable with one of us, all of us will always have the bond. We will never hurt you or judge you for what you need because we can feel your needs," Ocean said tightly with a hint of fear.

Daisy glanced up at him. Could she even be fair? She'd spent most of her life alone. She didn't feel worthy. She couldn't even swim. After making such a bizarre commitment to these beautiful, magical males, she needed to have them all close. They'd saved her life. "I could never push any of you out. That feels wrong." Daisy sighed. Life was a lot less complicated when Aerwyna was just River's very weird sister.

"You can have time," River said.

"I don't need time. I need -- I don't even know how to put it into words, but I need to feel you all close." She'd never expected they were anything but human. Incredibly buff and interesting humans, but not sea monsters or merpeople or whatever. And now they belonged to her. If she had to end up bonded or mated or whatever with three guys, at least they were easy on the eyes. What did she even do now? Did getting naked with her men have a proper order? *Her men.* She bit her lip. For someone as phobic of forever as she, Daisy couldn't believe this was happening. Hers? All of them?

"Mer mate for life. Your life force and ours are united." River's words haunted her. If he told her the truth, they'd die the same day she did. That made the commitment they made so much more intense. Could she make their sacrifice worth it?

"What about you guys?" She twisted her fingers nervously. "If I die and you don't take another female mate, you'll all die. Can you take multiple mates?"

River, her mind reader, brushed his fingers gently across her cheek as he cupped her face and she gazed up into his eyes. "We'll die. We've lived a long time, much longer than a human does. In all that time we've never found anyone as special as you. We're trusting you with all that we are. There's no way in hell we'd go looking for a backup."

Ocean grinned. When he touched her, some of her anxiety fell away. "Besides," he said, softly. "Even if we had a harem, the only one I'd trust to make me French toast is you. I don't want to live in a world without you."

"Are you using your mojo on me? Don't." Daisy hadn't meant to snap at him.

Ocean frowned. "If the ability that caused me so much pain can help you, why would you ask me to hold back?"

"People get anxious. It happens." Daisy forced herself to have the courage to look him in the eyes. "You can't just nullify that and expect me to be okay. I appreciate that you know I'm out of my comfort zone, but let me see if I can manage."

Both Ocean and River looked away from her. Daisy guessed River was probably in her head this whole time.

"I would never hurt you." Ocean turned to her again with that unnatural glow in his eyes. She'd seen it when he'd kept Kai from dragging her back into the water. "But with this new bond, your needs call to me. Asking me not to use *gift* for your benefit is as cruel as my using it without your consent. Forgive me."

Her righteous indignation crumbled like a

sandcastle in the surf. "Is my not being able to be mad at you part of the bond thing?"

Bayou chuckled. "We've all been in love with you since before we were smart enough to recognize it." He stroked his hand down her arm. "You're a once in a lifetime treasure. Don't worry about dying anytime soon. Our life force is part of you now and that comes with some protection. There's nothing more to worry about tonight."

"Is it so wrong to want to care for you?" Ocean brushed his fingers over her forehead and temples, working his magic. Anxiety fell away as she looked up at her three beautiful mates. Every self-conscious internal whisper quieted. As much as she wanted to resist, she closed her eyes and gave in to *gift*. Without the fears making her rethink the last twenty-four hours, the idea of three attentive guys with bodies that made her weak in the knees didn't sound so rough.

"What are you smiling about?" River asked as he looked down at her face.

"I was just thinking about what I plan to do to you all." Daisy giggled as she looked at her men crowding her on the bed. Those chiseled bodies took up a lot of space.

Bayou cupped her cheek.

"You know," River's tone rumbled with pure amusement and maybe a little joy. "He's going to be handsy, embarrassingly so, since you're the only woman he's ever been able to touch without causing pain."

"Dude, get out of my head." Bayou frowned.

"I hate it when he does that," Ocean said.

Daisy gazed up. Bayou and River circled the bed. They felt more like sharks than mer. Ocean's mojo was starting to wear off. She wasn't sure what to do so she just left them to guide the progression of this experience.

River made a quick gesture in her direction, and Ocean ran his hand so gently down her bare arm she shivered from the slight tickle. Once more that inner voice silenced. Ocean stood and started taking off his clothing. Bayou, then River followed. The men stood naked in her room. Feeling overdressed but entertained, she stretched out, watching her hunks. Their bodies were incredible. All that swimming had left them with extraordinary abs and arms. Frankly, their asses were nothing to overlook. She wished she could tell Sally. And then laughter burst from her as pure joy filled her heart. She'd been so broken for so long that she couldn't even deal with this level of happiness.

The guys all turned to her with confused scowls. And she laughed harder. "Sally," she gasped out.

"I don't want to know why *us* being naked has made you call out for your old boss." Bayou's reluctant statement didn't help her giggles.

She gulped in a breath. "Sally seriously had the hots for you guys because of the show. I can't even tell her that I get to sleep with *all* of you and we have like a mystical forever thing going on. Honestly, I'm not even sure what I'm going to tell her when she asks about my dating life."

"You're off the market," River growled and there was just enough menace to make her realize her mention of dating had riled him up a bit.

And that kept the smile on her face.

"Yes, it did," River said.

"Will there ever be a day that you learn about boundaries? What if I'm pissed off? Do you honestly want to see those thoughts clearly?" Daisy tried to look stern and did manage a glare for about three seconds.

"Lander, there isn't a single thought you could have that I don't want to see."

"Challenge accepted." She imagined worms and then old rotting worms, but they turned into cartoon characters with gray wigs and walkers in her head and she couldn't make them gross again.

"Hopeless," River muttered.

"If you two are done making a sacrilege of *gift*, I would like to get on with getting it on," Ocean teased.

All of their impressive cocks stood at attention and drew her eye to the lovely line-up.

She got off the bed and walked the gauntlet, running her finger lightly over the erections as she passed the men. Bayou sucked in a breath, but River and Ocean didn't give her the same satisfaction. She took River's cock in her hand and squeezed gently.

River took hold of the hem of her tank top and pulled it over her head. Her breasts bounced and both nipples tightened as the cool air hit her body. Ocean helped her undress and Bayou stood behind her. He slowly worked the fabric off her hips, letting the garment glide down her thighs to hit the floor. She kicked the clothing away.

"You have the best body in this room," Bayou whispered in her ear, making her shiver as his breath touched her skin.

Ocean ran a finger down her spine and then his hand rested on her ass. "I think she needs a good spanking. All that 'too brave for her own good' stuff today just about killed me." He lightly massaged her skin and then gave her a gentle slap.

Daisy laughed out a short shriek that turned into a giggle. "Hey now. Aren't we already being kinky enough here, at least by human standards? Geez."

"I suppose we'll have to ease you into the Triad." Ocean sat down as he rubbed her ass cheek where he'd smacked her. "When I thought I'd never see you again I lost my mind. I love you." He took a hold of her hips and pivoted her to sit facing him on his lap.

"Oof," she breathed, and her eyes widened in surprise. Ocean was quick, and strong. His cock pressed so close the hard length skimmed her belly. He moved his legs so that hers had to widen to keep her seated.

"Don't hurt her," Bayou warned. He came to stand behind her and put his hands on her shoulders, steadying her. His warm fingers massaged her shoulders. "Damn, I love touching you. I never thought -- not even with my kind --" There was a catch in his voice.

Chapter Ten

River took her breasts in his hands. His thumbs strummed her nipples.

Electricity shot through Daisy. She closed her eyes and sighed as she let her head fall back to rest on Bayou's arm.

"That feels so good. Are you using *gift*?" Daisy didn't know how she felt about them using their powers on her.

"Nope, but if you like that how about this?" Ocean ran his fingers between her folds and rubbed her clit.

She moaned.

"You're the gift," Bayou whispered in her ear before kissing her neck.

"She's wet. I think our Daisy likes our touch. Do you like it, sand dragon?"

"Yeah," she whispered. "I'm guessing there isn't much you could do I wouldn't like. Sand dragon?"

Ocean chuckled. "Today, standing in the surf with that driftwood, you were pretty fierce."

"Terrible nickname," River muttered. He sat on the bed and took her unoccupied nipple between his lips, dragging on it with enough force to elicit a moan from her.

Daisy opened her eyes and caught River, Ocean, and Bayou reflected in the mirror on the wall. The sight stole her breath. They surrounded her. For so long she'd been alone. Now she wasn't in a way that defied words. Bayou's gaze caught hers in the reflection. He smiled a slow, sensual smile before carefully tilting her head and moving her hair so that he could kiss the other side of her neck. He sucked her skin, just under her ear.

Ocean slid a finger inside of her. Then another. He found the perfect pace, pressing her G-spot each time he arched his fingers deep before flexing them back. He continued to rub his thumb against her clit. Daisy closed her eyes as the pleasure Ocean gave washed through her.

Bayou let go of the hair he'd been holding out of his way. The silky sensation slithered down her back. He took hold of the mass to twist the hair around his hand until he cupped the back of her scalp. He pulled forward just enough for him to have better access to her lips, but not enough to hurt her.

Daisy kissed him back, deeply. Bayou's tongue delved into her mouth. She let her head fall back and got lost in sensation. Helplessness hit her because of the way she dangled, positioned on Ocean's lap, but Bayou kept her steady. She fought a moment's terror over just how willingly she'd let these men become her anchor.

River and Ocean still caressed her, and she trembled a moment away from orgasm. Bayou kissed her with tender passion. She shattered. Moaning, Daisy let out a cry against Bayou's mouth as her pussy constricted around Ocean's fingers. Wave after wave rolled through her and she came hard for them.

River lay next to her. Watching her pleasure. Spent, she didn't protest when Bayou helped her lay back on the bed. He held her heartbreakingly gentle as he pressed a tender kiss to her mouth. He lay down next to her and his lips found hers. At first, his kiss stayed tender, but then he sucked her lower lip... hard. Erotic sensation shot through her body, all the way to her toes. Groaning, she let him part her legs with his thigh. She was so ready. Daisy helplessly wiggled her hips against him. He found her neck and kissed where her pulse thundered. Then he trailed his mouth to the swell of her breasts. He moved lower to suck one nipple hard, nipping before he moved to the other. He took his time with that one, lapping with tender affection until both were stiff, sensitive peaks. Daisy watched him torment her nipple, excitement gathering in her core. She desperately wanted one of the men to touch her clit again.

Bayou chuckled as if he sensed her impatience. He kissed his way down her stomach, twirling his tongue into her belly button, causing her to gasp. Then his lips found the mound just above her pussy. His tongue lapped at her intimate flesh. Her hips bucked and she whimpered. He moved his long arms and snaked them up her body. Bayou began to pinch and tease her nipples until her lust became a burning-sun-going-supernova. She gasped, close to coming. The ripples and contractions of pleasure rolled through her as she came, but then he pulled away.

A disappointed cry broke from her. "Please," she whimpered.

His large erection bounced as he knelt on the bed, taking her leg casually in his hands. He ran his hand from her hip to her ankle. When he reached her foot, he pressed a long, tender kiss into her instep and massaged her foot.

River stood to the side, stroking his clock. He nodded to Ocean. They moved closer, and each of them claimed one of her breasts. River sucked while Ocean fondled her. Ocean watched her face and grinned. She bit her lip.

"You're beautiful," he said.

Daisy closed her eyes and her hips bucked. She

wanted one of them to give her pussy some attention.

Bayou parted her legs wider and reached for her other foot. He kissed the second instep and repeated the massage, wringing a whine of pleasure from her, before he kissed his way back toward her wet, wanting pussy.

River gave her nipple a quick pinch. Bayou sucked her clit between his teeth, and she cried out. Bayou lapped at the nub, and she pressed her thighs gently against his head, arching up and grinding her pussy against his mouth.

"I'm so close." She gasped.

Ocean and River kept playing with her breasts. Bayou stuck his finger inside of her and found her G-spot. Then he added another digit. Bayou sucked her clit hard.

Daisy cried out a primal wail as her body quivered against Bayou's fingers. When he pulled them out, she whimpered.

"Because of you, my dead heart can beat again," Bayou said softly. "But River must be the first."

Bayou pulled her to him for a tender kiss. She could taste the musk of her own desire on his lips, but she didn't care. His kiss kindled her passion again. He let her go. She sensed his reluctance.

River knelt between her legs. Bayou and Ocean, higher on the mattress, played with her breasts.

"Fuck me, River," she pleaded in a soft, seductive tone as she looked up at him.

River groaned as he pressed his mouth against hers. She clung to him, tangling her fingers in his soft, dark hair. She kissed him back just as hard as he kissed her, and her eyes closed.

When he pulled away, she looked up into his face and fought her confusion.

"I can give you what you need, but first I have to know you're ours." River's gaze held hers. "Tell me you belong to our Triad," he demanded.

"Please, River," she begged.

"Tell me."

"I belong to you, all of you."

River made a sound that was something between a growl and a sigh.

He thrust forward, his cock sliding inside of her. The angle of his entry intensified the feeling, and she instantly surrendered to the raw need. All the amazing sensations caused her to shudder violently. She wrapped her arms around him, crying out with a single gasp.

Daisy rolled her hips with River inside of her. He moaned. He matched the rhythm she set, and he thrust deeply inside her core as she moved on him. She arched her back. "I'm so fucking close!" She looked up into his strained face, and when she came, she screamed.

"River!" Daisy shook with the force of the pleasure coursing through her. He pumped into her harder, and the orgasm kept going. River wrapped her hair around his hand and pulled her head back gently to kiss the skin at her throat. She was pliable and submissive as he kissed her neck, and she howled with the force of her release. Her pussy clenched, and she bucked against him.

River grunted. His passionate attention almost hurt as he kept going with relentless vigor. Daisy couldn't stop her keening wail, a mixture of great pleasure and emotional overload, as she came. He bucked a final time. His eyes closed. A long, purely male sound came from him. Daisy had never come this hard before. She whimpered. Her eyes fluttered shut, and she arched her back. Tears leaked out of the corners of her eyes as her orgasm died with a shudder; her passion was so blindingly intense she sobbed unintelligible sounds.

Ocean touched her shoulders gently and he rained kisses over her face. "It's okay," he murmured. "And we've only just begun."

"Are you sure she hasn't had enough?" Bayou's voice held both worry and regret.

"No, it -- it wouldn't be right to stop now." Something about this Triad stuff prompted her protest.

Ocean lay down next to her. He kissed her as he put his hand between her legs. She flinched and his touch grew gentler.

"Relax for me, Daisy," Ocean whispered.

She followed his direction and let go of a slow breath.

"That's it," he encouraged as he rubbed her clit. "Do you want me to stop?" he asked.

"No," Daisy admitted feeling a flush creeping up her neck. He leaned in to kiss her cheek. She wrapped her arms around his neck. He moved back and she let him go reluctantly.

He straddled her. She lay still, looking up at him and he sank into her slowly. Her pussy gripped him. Fire rekindled inside of her.

Ocean let out a long breath. "Fuck, that's good. That's really good."

She arched her back and her hips thrust up. He seemed to be holding back, going slow. The weird peace his touch inspired in her spread through her body. There was no soreness, only pleasure.

He peered down into her face, searching. "I will never cause you pain."

Ocean kissed her neck. He took one of nipples

into his mouth. Daisy cried out, and her pussy clung to him like a vise. The aftershocks of her first orgasm grew until she started to come again. He thrust into her, and the slow gentle pace increased until he thrust harder. Each stroke of his cock brought her more pleasure. She made little keening noises she'd never made before. Ocean groaned against her neck as he came. He held her tightly. This orgasm felt different than the powerful one she'd just had and yet equally satisfying.

But they hadn't finished yet. She turned her head to the side. Bayou lay watching her face.

"You too," she whispered. "You too."

Even as Ocean held her, his cock still inside of her, Bayou moved closer and kissed her. He darted his tongue into her mouth. She let him deepen the kiss, and his rough hands gripped her head. His fingers tangled in her hair.

Ocean traced her collarbone with his magic fingers.

Bayou groaned against her mouth, and she explored his warmth with her tongue. Her eyes closed and she let the security of Ocean's arms and Bayou's mouth lull her into a hypnotic trance. Her body hummed with awareness.

Ocean pulled out of her. Kissing her nipples and making her whimper against Bayou's mouth.

* * *

When Ocean moved out of his way Bayou held her arms down at the wrists and pulled back to look at her. Her hair spread out around her like the waves of the ocean and her eyes were half-shut. The swollen look of her lips only fired his blood. She lay docile under him. There lived a shimmer of anticipation in the way she gazed at him. Her breasts shuddered with the force of her panting breaths. Bayou ached.

"Tell me what you want."

"Please," she begged.

"No, tell me what you want and who you want it from."

"Bayou, please," she tried again.

"Not good enough," he chided.

"Bayou, I want you to… lick me."

"Where do you want me to lick, sweetheart?"

"My… pussy. Breasts. Everywhere. Please, Bayou, make me come again."

He loved the way the words rolled out of her mouth. His name on her lips was the most seductive of it all.

He started with her right nipple. She hissed and arched her back. She seemed to like it a little rough which turned him on as much as it seemed to excite her. She was the first woman he'd been able to touch like this. His past encounters had been tributes from his captors and had left him feeling monstrous. No matter how hard he'd tried to keep the darkness of *gift* from them his will wasn't enough. Daisy, the woman of his Triad, gave him a chance for happiness. The one woman he'd touched without fear.

When he gave the left nipple a tug, she cried out. Then she ground her pelvis against his hip. He could smell her musky readiness. Even after she'd taken the others, she wanted him. The musky perfume of sex filled the air as she thrashed under him. Seeing her so desperate made him ache.

He let go of her arms and kissed his way down her stomach until he found her mound. Bayou dropped a kiss there before dipping his head lower. He ran his tongue in her slit until he found her clitoris. Daisy wailed as he began lapping at her as quickly as he could. She moaned and wiggled as he pressed harder against her. Her body made her readiness clear, but the bond they all shared also told him what she needed.

"Bayou, fuck me!"

He couldn't say no. He pulled back to straddle her before sliding inside her with a single, hard thrust. Her velvet heat wrapped around him and she contracted, squeezing him tightly. The sensation forced a long, low moan from him. She whimpered, and her legs wrapped around his hips and buttocks. He thrust into her again.

She cried out; and bucked her hips to meet him. His beautiful Daisy went wild under him. Her ardent response only enhanced the experience. He couldn't hold back a second longer.

Bayou came inside of her. Her cry turned into whimpers by the time he collapsed beside her. He reached out and she didn't protest as he pulled her close. Bayou kissed her head. He'd kill to protect her. He'd die to make her happy. She meant more to him than all the treasure in all the kingdoms.

When he turned her to her side, she wrapped her arms around him. Her eyes fluttered closed, and she slept. Their sweet little maid, exhausted. He didn't let her go. Kai's legion could be lurking nearby, and he wouldn't risk leaving her alone.

Ocean put his hand on Bayou's shoulder. "Stay with her tonight. This bed isn't big enough for the four of us." He extracted himself from where he lay partially covering them both with his body.

Bayou pulled her tighter against him. He nodded. He didn't trust his voice to speak. He looked to River. The prince had more right to hold her than he did.

River grinned. "I trust you to keep her safe. I just hope you don't have to protect us from her in the morning. I hope she won't be angry when we don't all try to pile into this little bed. We'll have to see about getting her something bigger. I hope this won't be the last time she's willing to mate all of us at once."

Bayou understood his hope because he shared it. Still unable to speak, he only gave a single, firm nod.

After they left, hours passed before Bayou let himself sleep. Every moment she remained his and his alone was too precious to waste.

Chapter Eleven

Morning sun woke Daisy before her alarm. Bayou looked down into her face. His expression unreadable yet strangely heartbreaking.

"Good morning," she whispered in a rusty voice. She could use a strong cup of coffee.

"We're getting you a bigger bed," he said in his gruff way. "They wanted to be here."

Daisy couldn't stop the smile from spreading across her lips. "I'm not mad. This is a pretty tiny bed for such big guys. Thank you for staying with me. I slept well. I must have known I was safe and sound."

A flush darkened his high cheekbones. "Whatever. Hungry?"

"Always. I'll get up and make breakfast for everyone. Would you walk me to the house?"

He responded with just a grunt as he stood up and started looking for his clothing.

Daisy watched him. Her lips twitched as she tried not to grin. He couldn't fool her. This new connection they shared had grown exponentially since last night and she could actually feel how happy he was. "You're kind of cute when you're embarrassed."

"I am not!" He glared at her.

She giggled which only darkened his scowl.

She got up and hopped into the shower. She was sore, but the incredible soreness of a woman who'd been well loved. She hummed as she washed. Some sand remained in her hair from all the beach drama, so she shampooed twice. When she finally finished and dried off, she went into her room.

"Thought you might have drowned in there,

lander," Bayou grumbled.

Daisy tossed her towel at him as she grabbed a T-shirt and jeans out of the dresser. "You didn't have to wait for me."

He grunted again.

As much as he pretended he didn't care, she felt waves of protective concern radiating off him. This bond thing was going to be weird and maybe a little too honest. She pulled on some underwear and clasped her bra. He sat on the bed watching her. The hunger in his eyes brought her lust back to life. She cleared her throat and looked away. "I do know my way to the house. Seriously, if you have things to do --"

"No," he cut her off. "I've got time."

She pulled her T-shirt over her head and slipped into her jeans. She dug in the drawer and found her favorite socks. Never one to have amazing balance she almost toppled over as she leaned over to put one on.

Bayou had her upright before she realized she'd stumbled. "Give those here." He snatched away her socks and rolled the first one on her foot and then repeated the process on the bare one. "Don't fall on your ass."

Daisy's face burned. "I can put my own socks on. I've been doing it a long time."

He glanced up and for the first time she saw a genuine grin on his face. "Then you should be better at it."

Daisy made an outraged huff as he stood. He took her hand gently and his touch stole her annoyance. "Let's go." This time when he spoke to her the gruffness was gone. He pulled on his clothing.

She slipped on her shoes, without incident or assistance, and they left the cottage. The dewy grass felt cool against her sandaled feet as they made their way toward the house. The air smelled crisp. "It's chilly," Daisy said.

"Do you need a coat?" His tone hinted at concern.

"No. I'll live, and by the time I'm ready to come back to the cottage the sun will be out, and it'll warm up. You don't have to worry about me."

He grunted again.

Daisy slipped her arm around his waist and his hand tightened on hers. He might be a man of few words, but his actions spoke for him. When they arrived at the door he paused with his hand on the handle.

"Are you okay?" Daisy asked softly.

"I -- I love you." He opened the door and went inside without waiting for a response or looking at her. She stood staring at the closed door for a moment before recovering enough to go inside. This new bond thing told her the truth of his words but hearing them made her happy. River and Ocean's voices floated into the kitchen. They were talking by the offices. Humming off-key, she started to make breakfast. Eggs and bacon, stick-to-your-ribs lander food for her guys. *Her guys.* In the blink of an eye everything had changed. This bond made her feel like she belonged.

Daisy had all the food she wanted to make sitting out on the counter when she heard a commotion outside. She put down the pan she held and went to the window. A huge man with long gray hair and a scowl, draped in what looked like a wet silk cape and nothing else came stomping toward the house like he owned the island. A bunch of naked men surrounded him. They all carried what looked like spears.

Daisy shrieked.

River and Ocean came running into the kitchen.

"What happened?" River asked.

"Kai is back, or someone, and they have weapons!" Daisy scanned the room for anything she could use to fight.

River and Ocean exchanged glances. "It's okay," River said.

"Okay?" Daisy didn't think those guys looked okay.

The door flew open, and the caped guy stood glaring into the kitchen.

"Hello, Father," River said in a less than welcoming tone.

"*Father*?" Daisy was *so* not ready to meet the parents!

Mate to the Mermen (Mermen 2)
Ashlynn Monroe

Daisy Daniels never expected her temp job cleaning for three hunks on a private island would lead to romance. She clearly hasn't been watching enough reality TV. Falling in love with one, let alone all three, of the Watersons would be complicated enough without the burden of protecting their secret. Ocean, Bayou, and River aren't just celebrity treasure hunters, they're mermen.

Protecting the secret of her lovers is more challenging than Daisy ever imagined -- almost as challenging as learning to cook without the help of the Internet. Still, her life with the Triad would be perfect if River's father, the King of Atlantis, didn't hate her, and if Kai, the Prince of the Aegeans, wasn't constantly causing trouble.

When karaoke night reveals Daisy has *gift* she has a lot more to think about than the laundry. Saving the world was never in the job description. How can she risk using her newfound *gift* when she could harm the three people she loves most?

Chapter One

River swore under his breath. He hadn't expected his father to show up. The old man's timing couldn't have been worse. In the upheaval of the last twenty-four hours, they'd missed an important call about a dive. That job couldn't have come at a ghastlier time. They needed the footage, but the wreck wasn't in Aegean-controlled currents. When they'd decided to dive it, they'd had no idea how complicated their lives would become. He turned to Daisy. "This is my father, King Delta, the ruler of Atlantis." He returned his attention to his father. "Father, this is Daisy. She's my Triad's mate."

Father snorted a rude, almost dismissive, sound. "A *human*?" Father spoke out loud, but in Atlantean. "Why are you so intent on destroying my faith that you'll rule? I have given you time to come to your senses, but I'm starting to lose patience."

River bristled. He replied in English. "I will not allow you to disrespect my mate."

Daisy put her hand on River's arm. "It's okay."

He could see the compassion in her beautiful brown eyes. "No, it's not." River put his arm around Daisy. Ocean and Bayou moved to stand at his side.

King Delta sighed. "I see you and your Triad are in agreement," he continued in Atlantean, excluding Daisy.

"We are," River said. "Triad always."

"The seal must be found." Father glared at Daisy a moment before turning his attention back to River. "I can't believe you were so weak as to allow that pathetic excuse for a male to come into your home and take what belongs to our kingdom." He glanced at Ocean and Bayou. "For all your talk of Triad, they've done nothing to help you protect our legacy." He pinned River with an intense look filled with authority and anger. "River, you and you alone were entrusted with the seal as my way to ensure you remembered your responsibilities. Instead, you have mated with a human and let Prince Kai walk away with a national treasure. What do you have to say for yourself?"

River's throat tightened. Even as ridiculous as his father looked standing on land in nothing but a cape, he still bore his position with an aura of power. He could still make River feel like nothing with a glance. If he tried to explain that Daisy would have died if he'd gone after the artifact, would his father relent? Probably not. "I'm sorry, Father."

"*Sorry* will not get the seal back. *Sorry* will not change the fact you tied your soul to a frail human. What are you going to do, my son?" Father crossed his arms over his chest.

"We will help River get the seal back," Ocean assured the king.

Father's brow creased as he regarded Ocean with disgust. "I was not talking to you, traitor."

River scowled. "Ocean would give his life for me and for our kingdom. He is not a traitor."

King Delta turned to Bayou. "And did you want the human too, monster? Couldn't you have talked sense into your prince? You know how easily the vulnerable are destroyed. You know how weak a human is, and yet you would allow your prince to tie you all to one female's short life?"

Bayou glared at the king. "She has the strength of a Triad now."

Few would have had the courage to do the same.

River's throat tightened.

"You are all pathetic!" The king growled, shaking his fist at River. "If the law allowed me to give the throne to your sister, I would. If you do not regain the seal, I'll have my army drag those criminals you bonded with to the deepest, darkest prison in Atlantis. I'll make sure they stay alive, but in hellish misery."

Ocean and Bayou both stiffened. River looked away, unable to meet the anger and shame Father directed at him. "Father, please, don't say such things. Daisy is human and you might disapprove of my decision to form our Triad but doing that would be beneath you. A king should never seek personal vengeance. You've told me that many times."

His father took a step closer to him. He raised his fist. "You dare --"

Daisy stepped closer to the king. "I don't know what you're saying to them but chill out."

King Delta turned his attention away from River to glare at Daisy. "*Chill out?*" he parroted in heavily accented English.

"Yes," she said. "Chill. These are amazing men, and your tone is clear no matter what language you're speaking. They don't deserve a lecture. This is their home. If you can't be respectful, maybe you should leave."

River, Ocean, and Bayou inhaled sharply in unison. No one had ever dared tell King Delta to leave before now.

"I will not do this *chill out*! Fool human! You are of weak thoughts. You give yourself to these males, but they are little fish. Weak fish." King Delta's chin rose as he narrowed his eyes at Daisy.

"Let me assure you, there's nothing little about these fish." Daisy rolled her eyes and a small chuckle escaped. She looked to River, and he could see love in her gaze. "They are strong and brave."

The king's guard wore heavy tunics that fell to their knees. River was glad for Daisy's sake that they were mostly covered as the large men approached her. Bayou was the first to make a protective move toward Daisy. The guards, knowing full well how easily Bayou could destroy their minds with *gift*, all stopped.

Daisy glared at the king of Atlantis, causing River to catch his breath in fear for her. "Who's the little fish now? You need all these big guys to protect you from a human woman's words?"

The king gave a derisive snort, but he held his hand up to stay his guard. In Atlantean he said, "Don't bother with this unarmed human. She's no threat to us." Then he looked at Daisy and returned to speaking English. "Your tongue is sharp, female. But in water you have no protection from my wrath. Stay dry, woman of my son's Triad, for under the waves my anger is great." He turned, his cape billowing dramatically, then motioned for his guard to follow. His entourage tripped over themselves in their haste.

River was quiet as he watched them go. Bayou had moved to put his arm around Daisy. When they were gone Daisy turned to look at her Triad. She tilted her head to the side as her brow furrowed. "What? Why are you all so pale?"

Bayou stepped back to scowl at her. He started to pace. "That was fucking stupid. If you see River's father again, keep your mouth shut."

Daisy sucked in a sharp breath. Her lips pursed angrily, and her gaze shifted on Bayou with wrath. River put his arm around her, tugging her close. He picked up her long brown braid and tickled her nose with it. Her soft, sensual giggles broke the tension.

When she looked up into his face, he had to kiss her. His lips caught hers and his kiss was hungry, needy.

No one else had ever spoken up for him like she had. She'd had no idea just how dangerous her actions were, but that blind need to protect his heart fed his need to be close to her. When he broke the kiss, he put his cheek on the top of her head. "Brave and foolish. You're perfect for us."

"I don't know what he was saying, but I didn't like the way you guys -- felt. It's so weird how clearly I feel your emotions now." Daisy looked over his shoulder at Ocean and Bayou.

River sighed. "We were more worried about you than ourselves." He pulled back to look into her face. "Daisy, my father is dangerous."

"I know. I felt it too. You all fear him. It makes me dislike him, a lot!"

He let her go and stepped back to look at her. "Your unity with us will be a learning curve for us all. Promise me you'll never speak harshly to my father again. He might not have power on land, but in the sea that changes. I don't want anything to happen to you."

Her brow furrowed. "If I die, you die." Through the bond, River felt the moment the realization hit her that if she went too far, she'd put all their lives in danger. Her recklessness was no longer her own, and she wasn't comfortable with the knowledge. "Would your father let that happen to you?"

He loved her flame but hated her willingness to step into the fire. He also wanted to assure her he wasn't angry, because he felt her fear that she'd hurt his pride. "There are things that are worse than death. Each of us would willingly take risks with ourselves, but it's different for us now. Just know that we love you. You are part of our souls now. We are one."

Scaring her was the last thing he wanted, but something had to be done. He'd seen his father's darkest side during the war, but he hoped Daisy never would. Even if he was the heir, his father hated him for the Triad. He saw River's compassion as weak. Father had no idea it was also what had made him strong enough to find happiness and build this life.

Ocean cleared his throat. He pushed his shaggy blond hair out of his all too knowing expression in his blue eyes. "Now that the company has left, I think it's time we headed to the mainland. We'd planned to go for supplies today and it couldn't hurt to let the island air out from the stinking bad vibes left behind from His Royal Pain in the Ass's visit. We could all use a little fun."

"Maybe I'll stay home," Bayou grumbled.

"Please come." Daisy stepped away from River to put her hand on Bayou's arm.

He glanced up at her sharply, and some of the darkness in his expression vanished. He put his hand over Daisy's. "I don't know." He let out an exasperated sigh.

Daisy grinned at him. "Please! Sally will be so excited to meet you all. And Ocean is right, we deserve some fun after the last twenty-four hours."

"Fine," Bayou huffed.

River crossed his arms and studied their woman for a moment. Daisy was good for them.

* * *

Sally stood in the doorway to The Wharf, wearing a huge grin. Daisy squealed and rushed over to her. She hadn't realized how much she'd missed her friend until now. The smell of stale beer and popcorn filtered out to mingle with the seaside breeze.

"I see they didn't murder you."

Daisy smiled back. The bar, and Sally, hadn't changed a bit, and somehow that surprised Daisy because she'd changed so much in a week. How could the rest of the world just keep going on like nothing had happened, when everything she understood about herself and the planet had shifted? It took her a moment to regain her composure. "Nope." A hot flush crept up her neck making her self-conscious. "They've been great." She couldn't explain her new relationship without endangering their secret.

The Wharf was busy because it was karaoke night.

"Great, huh?" Sally saw too much. A curious expression tilted her lips up at the corners as one brow rose.

Daisy threw her arms around Sally. "I've missed you."

"I've picked up my phone to call you so many times I've lost count," Sally admitted. "I've had so many regrets sending my best friend into a vacuum of communication silence."

"I know the feeling." Daisy let go of Sally and opened the door to the bar. "The first round is on me."

"I'll never turn down a free drink." Sally chuckled as she followed Daisy inside. Karaoke hadn't started yet. The DJ waved to them as he finished setting up. "How long before you're back on hunk island?" There was a sparkle of mischief in her blue eyes as she smiled, causing a crinkle at the corners.

Daisy's flush burned hotter. "They're meeting me here. I promised them we'd do a duet."

Now Sally flushed. "I'm not singing in front of those manly men! How do I look?"

Daisy giggled. She held up two fingers toward Angela, the bartender. "Liquid Courage." Daisy handed Sally the first of the two tap beers that Angela sat in front of her. "You're absolutely adorable and sexy, lady!"

She was. Sally was wearing the cutest top with a jean jacket and a pair of artistically ripped skinny jeans. Her graying blond hair was up in a twist.

"It will take more than this." Sally frowned. "I'll buy the next round."

"I warned them we were terrible," Daisy assured her friend. "They just want to meet you. I think they're happy you talked me into taking the job. It's working out better than I'd hoped. They're great. Each one of them is special in his own way. I've never felt as at home anywhere as I feel on the island." She pressed her lips together and looked away, unable to meet Sally's eyes. "Thank you."

Sally almost choked on her beer. "Scoop! There's something going on between you and one of them, isn't there? I've never seen you blush talking about a guy before."

Daisy hadn't touched her drink. She realized she didn't want anything to loosen her lips. Immediately a wave of protective concern washed through her. The bond she shared with her Triad felt almost sacred. As much as she loved Sally, she wouldn't jeopardize the guys by giving away anything about who they really were. Telling Sally, she was bonded -- mated -- whatever with all three of them would certainly raise questions she didn't want to tackle. "They're good guys. Please, let's leave it at that."

Sally pouted. "I wouldn't judge you, sweetie. If I was twenty years younger, I'd probably start something with all three of them."

Daisy didn't know if she should giggle or cry. Sally was the closest thing she had to family, and she wanted to tell her the truth. If another human could understand and be happy for her, it was Sally. But she couldn't risk compromising the Triad. "I don't know if they could handle Sassy Sally."

They found a table by the stage and sat down. Sally took a sip of her drink and chuckled. "As long as Dangerous Daisy doesn't burn down their house with her cooking, the agency's reputation remains intact." She paused and gave Daisy a long, scrutinizing look. "Whichever one is lucky enough to end up with her better make sure they treat her well or he will suffer my vengeance!"

"Don't worry about me, Sal. Seriously, I'm sure none of them would ever hurt me. I -- I'm happier than I've ever been."

Sally sipped her drink, eyeing Daisy. She opened her mouth as if to say something when the door opened, but then stopped to gape. Everyone in the bar turned to stare at the three men entering.

Daisy turned to see her Triad arrive. River led the group into the bar. His long black hair and dark brown eyes were beautiful. His black goatee was perfectly groomed, as usual. Everything about him radiated strength and power. Her heart fluttered with pride. Her Triad was striking. Bayou was lanky and tall. His dark hair had a messy kind of style that always seemed intentional even if it wasn't. Ocean's blond All-American boy/mer good looks contrasted well with the others. They filled the small, dark space with their presence. Only her guys could own a room like that.

River noticed her and headed in her direction.

Daisy didn't miss the envious glances from other women. She also enjoyed a rare moment with her friend. Sally was speechless. Sally was never speechless.

River extended his hand toward Sally. "I'm River," he said.

She nodded and took his hand limply. "I -- I -- Wow."

Daisy chuckled. "She's your biggest fan. She made me watch the show all the time. Nothing personal, but I spent most of my time scrolling through social media instead of watching. I've never been a big history buff."

Ocean sat down. "Thank you," he said to Sally. "Our fans make our work possible. We'll convince Daisy of the importance of what we do." He winked at Sally and gave her such a striking smile he should have auditioned for toothpaste ads.

Sally's response was an unintelligible gurgle as she gazed starry eyed at Ocean.

Daisy smiled with such genuine delight that she had to take a breath and just enjoy the moment. A week ago, she'd have never been able to imagine this meeting.

Bayou took the seat closest to Daisy, but far enough away from other humans to avoid anyone accidentally encountering his gift. His tension was palpable through the bond they shared. His movement broke the spell Ocean held over Sally, and she glanced at him. She flinched quickly but managed to recover in time to cover with a polite nod. Through the bond Daisy felt the sadness his darkness caused him. Even a human could feel how hazardous being near him was. It hurt him, but Daisy also could feel that he didn't resent Sally for it.

Daisy's heart ached for him. "Would anyone like my drink?" Daisy offered, trying to distract Bayou. "I'm not really thirsty for alcohol. I'm going to grab a water."

Sally jerked toward Daisy and the incredulous look on her face made Daisy laugh. "That island air must really be something. I might have to visit you out there some time."

Daisy squeaked in alarm.

Ocean reached out and patted her arm. "Daisy's friends are welcome anytime. We just need to know in advance. Surprise visitors have never been something we're comfortable with."

Sally glanced down at the hand on Daisy's arm. A grin broke across her face and she glanced between Ocean and Daisy. "Oh, for sure. Of course. You guys," and when she said "you" she looked very intensely at Ocean with her brows raising and her posture leaning toward him, "are treating my Daisy okay, right?"

Jealousy rippled through the bond in Ocean's direction. Bayou's darkness grew and something about River's energy dimmed. Ocean removed his hand so quickly Daisy was almost hurt. He cleared his throat. "Yes, certainly. We've never had such a good housekeeper. She's efficient and very considerate. I'm sure we'll employ her for many years to come." He sat up a little straighter. "We're all very glad to have such a professional."

Sally shrugged one shoulder in his direction. "How's her cooking?" There was a silly slyness in the tone as she looked at Ocean. It was clear to Daisy that her friend was trying to figure out exactly how close she and Ocean were.

"Terrible," Bayou grumbled.

They all turned to look at him.

Daisy wasn't even sure what to say. She was trying to keep Sally from being suspicious, but after that, Ocean's compliment sounded faker than a three-dollar bill.

Bayou chuckled. The tension that had been growing through the bond stretched tighter. Daisy could feel the others suffering as much fear as she was about what he'd say next. "But hell, nobody's perfect. She's definitely not the worst housekeeper we've ever had. Your agency did a damn good job finding us someone."

River picked up the beer in front of Daisy and took a long drink. "I haven't had a beer in a bar in a long time. I'll get us the next round." He turned a breathtaking smile on Sally. She flushed like a teenager and looked away. "Daisy has told us about how much she enjoys coming here with you. When are you two going to dazzle us with your performance?"

Daisy chuckled. "Dazzle -- traumatize. Tomato -- tomahto. They'll start soon."

A casual peace returned to the bond as Sally settled back into her chair and took another sip of her drink. "We're terrible," she confessed. "I hope my Daisy hasn't filled your head with unreasonable expectations."

"Never," River said. "We expected warm beer and terrible singing."

Sally laughed. "And you're funny too. Wow. I do really love your show. I -- I can't believe you guys are here, at The Wharf of all places!"

Ocean laughed. "How could we stay away from our biggest fan? Daisy told us we have you to thank for her accepting the job. She's perfect for us." The way he said it didn't help disguise the relationship. Sally glanced between Ocean and Daisy again. "Daisy will never be mistreated or harmed with us. We all value her."

Sally put her beer to her lips and took a gulp

instead of a sip. "All of you?"

Daisy ignored the quick curious glance from her friend.

"He's just being nice. Ocean likes my French toast. I swear anyone would have probably worked out for them as well as I did. There's nothing special about me, Sal." Daisy decided it was time for a distraction. "Oh look! Is Jasmin going to sing?"

Sally glanced over to the table across from them, and Daisy let go of the breath she'd been holding. *Distraction accomplished.*

The DJ called for sign-ups, and Sally went to sign herself and Daisy up for a duet. River and Ocean got up and came back with a round of drinks. Water for Daisy, as requested.

Sally waved at one of the other agency people and Daisy watched her go over to chat with the woman. Now was her chance to scowl at her Triad. Daisy leaned over to whisper to the guys. "I'm trying to keep our arrangement on the DL."

"The DL?" Ocean asked.

"*Down low,*" Daisy whispered.

Ocean's brows drew together. "Are you ashamed of our bond?"

Daisy felt his uncertainty, like a zap, through the bond. "No, but I don't want Sally asking questions I'm not able to answer. I'm trying to protect you." She glanced around making eye contact with each of the men. "All of you. And stop with the jealousy. Of course a human would expect me to only be with one of you. From now on, just let her make whatever assumption she needs to make."

Sally returned and settled back in her chair. "We're all signed up to go. Fifth spot, right after Jasmin."

"Are you sure that's a good idea?" Daisy asked. "Jasmin can actually sing,"

Sally nodded enthusiastically. "I think I might be getting better. I'll help us pull this off."

Once the singing started, everyone enjoyed their drinks and the company. Ocean went and got another round as the third song began. Daisy asked for soda. She didn't trust herself. The urge to tell Sally how happy she was hovered on the tip of her tongue. She found herself laughing more than she had in a long time. Celebration of just being here with these people filled her soul to the brim. They were having a great time. Tonight was perfect.

And then it was their turn.

Daisy regretted inviting the guys to karaoke when she saw the song Sally picked.

"Don't Go Breaking My Heart? Really, Sal?"

"It's perfect. And I'm sending a message to your hunks."

Daisy rolled her eyes. The bond she had with the guys was a warm security blanket. She couldn't really describe how good it was just to be in the same room with them. She wasn't worried they'd break her heart in the way a human guy -- or guys -- might, but she was afraid of what forces might drive them away and back to where they'd come from. How would she survive that day?

She realized she did need to let Sally in on some of what was going on, but now didn't feel right. She'd give thought about how best to approach this when she returned to the island. Without a friend, if she lost them, she'd be too alone to bear the agony.

River gave her the thumbs up. Ocean winked. Even Bayou was smiling. She had time to figure it out. She wasn't losing anyone tonight.

Daisy accepted the mic Sally handed her. They took their places, and the music began. The lyrics scrolled on the prompter. Daisy and Sally sang.

Only a few words into the song Daisy noticed her guys wore pained expressions. By the time they'd finished the first chorus it was clear something was terribly wrong. Daisy glanced between the guys and the song scrolling on the screen. Sally didn't appear to notice, but through the bond she shared she sensed their agony.

Ocean fell off his chair. River held his head. Bayou left the bar.

Daisy dropped her microphone with a reverberating discordant clatter that blared out the speakers. She jumped off the stage and rushed to where Ocean lay and dropped to her knees, taking his head in her lap. He'd taken away her pain, too many times to count, and she could do nothing for him. Helplessness weighed on her. He seemed to be recovering, albeit slowly. "He drank too much," Daisy lied to concerned onlookers. "Ocean," she said softly. "I'm here. What can I do?"

Sally gave the DJ her mic and left the stage before the song was done. "What happened?" she asked when she was close to the table.

River and Daisy helped Ocean up off the floor.

"Too much to drink." Daisy couldn't look Sally in the eyes. "He -- he doesn't handle alcohol well."

"He didn't have that much. Did he start before they got here?" Sally's brow furrowed. "Is he okay?"

"Yeah," Daisy lied again. "They started early. You guys drank at The Seabird, right?"

River nodded. "Sure." His voice was strained.

"I think we should get him back to the island." She gave her friend a quick hug. "I'll see you soon."

"It's too bad you have to go. It's so early. The Seabird sells crappy drinks, so no wonder he's sick." Sally looked dubious. She was shrewd and not easily fooled. Ocean hadn't been keeping up with the others. He'd only finished one drink, giving several of his to Bayou.

"Don't worry. Everything is going great on the island. I'll talk to you soon. Stay, enjoy the night. We'll do it again, just you and me." River threw a wad of money on the table.

Sally nodded, watching them go.

Daisy let go of the breath she'd been holding unconsciously as they stepped out into the fresh, evening air. The next time she saw her friend she'd have a lot to explain. She just hoped she'd have it figured out by then.

Chapter Two

Bayou was pacing. When he saw them come outside, he glared at Daisy. "What the hell was that?" he practically shouted. He quickly put himself in check. Yelling at the woman he loved wouldn't do any of them any good.

"What?" Daisy widened her eyes.

Bayou sensed nothing malicious in her manner or tone. He felt her confusion through the bond. "That sonic pitch? Why would you attack us?"

A woman walking past gave them an odd look. Bayou glared at her, and she picked up her pace to scurry away. He waited until she was out of earshot. "Your voice -- your horrible, terrible voice was the most painful thing I've ever heard."

"Shh," Daisy said. "Keep your voice down. What do you mean, attack you?"

Bayou took her place and helped River with Ocean. "The singing. Your voice. You could have killed us."

"Killed you?" Daisy gasped. "I'd never kill you."

River groaned. "My head is throbbing. We'll talk about it at home."

Tears pooled in Daisy's eyes. "I told you we were bad."

Bayou hated how deeply he'd hurt her with his words, but she'd have made one hell of a mer assassin. He wanted to say something to apologize, but his head was still throbbing, and his stomach hurt. Every muscle in his body ached. Ocean's *gift* had to make this hardest on him. Would he recover? Fear for Ocean made his shock turn to anger. "You weren't just bad.

You were irresponsible. How could you have *gift* and not tell us? I know something about shame over the power the gods grant you, but this was a shitty way to show us."

"Show you?" Daisy choked out. "I -- I didn't do anything on purpose. I wasn't trying to show you anything. I don't know what happened in there. I -- I'm sorry." She covered her eyes with the palms of her hands and her shoulders shook silently.

Ocean seemed to be coming around more thoroughly. "You slayed in there, sand dragon."

"Terrible nickname," River muttered.

Bayou grunted.

"I'm sorry," Daisy whispered. "I -- I'd never hurt you on purpose. Humans don't have *gift*."

Bayou regretted lashing out. "Maybe not all of them, but you sure as hell do."

River cleared his throat. "We all know she didn't do this to hurt us. Take a moment and feel the bond. Stop being a bastard and just calm down. We'll figure this out. For the time being, no karaoke."

Daisy nodded.

When Bayou looked at her, she wouldn't meet his eyes. Guilt filled him. He knew what it was like to hurt someone unintentionally with *gift* and what it was like to hurt someone using *gift* as a weapon. He felt no intention when he reached out with the bond for Daisy. She was suffering.

"Forgive yourself," Bayou grumbled. He wished he had the same way with words River and Ocean had. They'd never be able to explain to the burden of a dark *gift* like he could, but he didn't have the strength to express what she needed to hear. He was a worthless mate. His gloom swirled around in his head until he wanted to scream. The boat came into view. He shut himself away from the others and pushed the bond down. He didn't want to drag the others into his despair, and he didn't want to feel the echoes of Daisy's pain. They were too similar to his own.

* * *

Daisy couldn't enjoy the beautiful sunset on the boat trip home. *Home.* She was already thinking of the island as her home. Her guilt over the guys' karaoke nightmare kept her spirits down. Tears prickled her eyes. The very idea that Bayou could think she'd hurt him -- them -- stung far worse than his acknowledgment of her severe lack of talent.

Ocean came over and sat down next to her. "Hey. Cheer up. I'm feeling better."

Daisy gave him a half-smile. "I'm glad. I'm so sorry about what happened back there. I had no idea my voice could have that effect on you."

Ocean offered her a bag. "I'm going to give you something I picked up for you in town, but I've got to ask you to promise not to make me regret it."

When Daisy looked inside, she didn't know if she should laugh or cry. "Thanks for this," she muttered, pulling the radio out of the bag.

"You mentioned you missed music and couldn't play it since we don't have internet at home. I'm really glad I didn't buy you the karaoke machine." Ocean reached over and took her hand. "On the bright side, you're not without protection against Kai. If that bastard shows up, sing your heart out, sand dragon. I wanted to give this to you now to show you that I trust you. I know this was not intentional."

This time when she smiled, it was genuine. "Thanks. I will only sing to Kai."

Ocean got up and went below.

The cool breeze hit her face and the fresh salt air

perked her up a bit. He'd bolstered her spirit more than he could know. He was right, she had a weapon. A very unique and secret weapon against the Aegeans. If Kai showed up on the island again, he'd regret it.

As the island came into view, Daisy was relieved. She'd never thought the first time she'd arrived here just how much she'd love it. Town had felt weird, even as small as it was, too people-y after getting used to the island's solitude. She hadn't picked up much for herself while they were on the mainland, and she'd completely forgotten the radio. Her guys were thoughtful. Maybe they could build a life even if they were so different. She just had to be careful with her newfound *gift*.

But what if she forgot and started to sing as she worked? What if one of them got hurt? Maybe she should see if there was some way she could break her bond with the Triad. She should leave so she'd never accidentally hurt them.

Ocean came over and sat down next to her. He kissed her temple. "It's okay. We trust you."

Daisy glanced up at him caught between feeling violated he was in her head and comforted that he understood her needs. She shrugged.

River moored the boat and they docked.

Bayou had been quiet on the ride home, but when she went to step off the boat, he was right at her side making sure she didn't fall. He took her hand as she stepped onto the gangway. "Thanks," she said softly. "I thought you were mad at me."

"I am mad, but only at myself. Sorry I snapped at you." Bayou's grip was comforting and firm as they made their way to the dock.

"You had every right. I should have -- I don't know -- made sure karaoke was something we could all do together. I keep having to remind myself you guys aren't human."

Bayou made a strange noise.

Daisy glanced up into his face. "What?"

"Our feelings for you are better than you'd ever get with some human guy. Don't go thinking you need a human male."

Was he jealous? That brooding hunk was actually worried she'd go looking for someone else when she had three devoted men? Daisy chuckled.

Bayou glared.

"Don't worry. You guys have ruined me for every other man on the land or in the sea. I -- I just don't want to hurt you by accident. Is there a way for me to break off my connection with you guys? I'm sure the last thing you'd want is a dangerous mate."

Bayou grunted. "You think I'm not dangerous? You're like me now in a way the others won't get. I'm sorry we have to share a burden like that. *Gift* can be beautiful, but I've never seen anything but the ugliness of mine. Mating with us has surely changed you. You're right, humans don't have *gift*. If you must blame someone, blame us. You're kind. I should never have said what I said."

Through the bond she felt something in him lighten. And that made her smile. "You have someone to understand now. If you're ever suffering from doubts about yourself, I'm here to talk. Always."

Bayou glanced back at the boat. "I'd better help them with the supplies. You might as well wait in the house. I want to be sure I get to kiss you goodnight, so don't go hiding yourself away in the cottage, okay?"

His words thrilled her. "You really still want to kiss me after I gave you a potentially fatal rendition of a terrible, dated song?"

"Yes. And I'm not afraid of you. I'm also not going to get on your bad side." He barked out a laugh. "Hell, we ought to be glad about this. You have something to protect yourself from Kai now."

"Ocean said the same thing," Daisy admitted.

"You're not defined by your *gift*. If anyone knows that to be true, it's me. Just don't dwell on it. Promise me."

"I promise."

He nodded and returned to the boat to help the others.

Daisy almost skipped up the hill and to the main house. Even after she'd crippled them with her siren song, they still wanted her. Had anyone ever accepted her like that before? Maybe just Sally. Through the bond, she knew they weren't ready to send her packing. There was a confidence in that solid connection she'd never had in another relationship. For someone phobic of commitment it was surreal to be so sure about her place in their family. *Family*. For the first time in as long as she could remember that word held meaning.

She unlocked the door and went inside.

"Hello, flower lander."

Daisy shrieked and almost dropped her bag with the radio inside. She whirled. Aerwyna sat at the table in the twilight shadows of the kitchen. "You almost gave me a heart attack. How did you get in here?" Daisy sat her bag on the counter.

Aerwnya stood. "Brother gave me a key." Her long reddish-brown hair had pearls and shells woven into the tresses hanging in waves down to her knees. "I'm sorry I attacked your heart. I hide key and lander clothing in the rocky place." Her dark eyes, so much like River's, sparkled with mischief. The princess of

Atlantis was as beautiful on the outside as she was on the inside.

"Your dad visited this morning. I don't think I like him."

Aerwyna chuckled. "Father has not friended you either. He has had plans for River and humans don't float in those currents."

Daisy turned on the lights. Hearing her deepest fears voiced by another, even one who had a bit of a language gap, was rough. "I've never wanted to swim in anyone's currents before."

Aerwyna stood straighter and brightened. "I bring gifts of currents to you."

"Huh?" Daisy was following her less than usual.

"Here. A gift." Aerwyna came closer to show Daisy a beautiful pendant. The jewelry was constructed of sea glass and pearls on a long golden chain.

"It's beautiful," Daisy said. "But I don't need a gift." Maybe Aerwyna was trying to say thank you for her part in keeping Kai from succeeding in kidnapping her?

"You do!" Aerwyna scrunched up her face. "This will give you the mer. This will let you enjoy River's currents. It's a precious thing. I stole it from Father."

"You stole it? I definitely can't accept something stolen." Daisy tried to push Aerwyna's hands away, but the mermaid was surprisingly strong as she put the chain around Daisy's neck.

"You must have. You need the currents. Father has the mer." Aerwyna stopped Daisy when she tried to take the necklace off. "Surprise River and swim the currents."

"I don't know how to swim," Daisy admitted. "Remember Kai trying to drown me?"

Aerwyna laughed her shrill dolphin-like sound. "You will try, but with this you will do it, like magic."

"I don't want you to get in trouble. I don't need a thank you gift, or whatever this is supposed to be. Like you said, your dad hasn't friended me. If he discovers you took something of his and gave it to me that won't endear me to him." Daisy sighed heavily. How could she make this woman understand?

"You don't need to be a deer for him. He will friend you when you're mer and he sees. You are a good human housekeeper and good mate to River. Please wear the mer or I will be sad." Aerwyna wrapped Daisy in a too-tight hug. The mer were crazy strong.

Daisy managed to wiggle away before she was bruised. "Okay, if you're sure you won't get in trouble and that I really need this. I'll wear it so I always have you close to my heart." She patted the center of her chest where the pendant rested.

Aerwyna smiled. She picked the pendant up and dropped it down the front of Daisy's shirt. "You will surprise River with your mer. And then you will tell me about his funny face."

When Aerwyna's expression lit up excitedly it was almost impossible to disappoint her. "Okay. I'll even take a picture if I get the chance."

Aerwyna clapped her hands. "You day my made!"

"Don't you mean I made your day?"

Aerwyna shrugged.

River walked in. He grimaced when he saw Aerwyna. "Hello sister."

"Don't be wrinkled forehead with me, brother. Father had to know."

River sighed. "Yeah, you're right. It's not your

fault Father was being Father. What brings you to land?"

"Girl talk," Aerwyna said. She winked at Daisy.

River glanced between them, and even without activating their bond Daisy could see he was curiously concerned about what his sister meant.

"She just wanted to thank me for my attempt to keep Kai from dragging her off." Daisy smiled at him. "Or maybe she wanted to be sure I'm keeping you guys on your toes."

Bayou and Ocean entered, smiling when they saw Aerwyna. "Hey there, princess," Ocean greeted her. "Daisy tried to kill us today."

Aerwyna laughed her shrill laugh. "Good. You need a woman to keep you remembering you're alive. Not killing you will make you alive."

"Something like that," Bayou muttered. He reached out and pulled Daisy into his arms and kissed her breathless. When he let her go, she stumbled back a bit. He steadied her. "Good night." He left the room without another word.

"That one." Aerwyna pointed to Bayou's retreating form. "Kill twice. I leave you to your sleep. Safe currents."

"Safe currents to you sister," River said as she left.

Daisy was left alone with River and Ocean. "I'm sorry about today."

"Stop worrying about it," River said. "It's actually good to know you have a way to keep Kai from hurting you. And this will be an interesting story to tell our grandchildren."

Daisy went hot, then cold. *Grandchildren?* Could humans and mermen have kids? Did she want merkids? How would a family work in their Triad dynamic? And really, after all the trauma of today, he dropped that on her? "*Could* we have kids?" she asked.

River cleared his throat. "It's been a long day. That's a conversation best had another time."

Daisy scowled, ignoring his suggestion they wait to talk about it. "Seriously, can we?"

"Yes, if the old legends are correct, we can." River looked away, but Daisy noticed the flush coloring his high cheekbones. "If you want, I guess."

She didn't know how to respond.

Ocean chuckled. "I'm tired too, but not so tired I wouldn't mind practicing that whole baby making thing."

River rolled his eyes. "I know you like the cottage, but I don't like the idea of you being out there alone when we don't know when or if Kai will make another move. Remember when you asked about that empty room upstairs? We'd left it unfinished in case we ever found a mate. Would you consider moving into the main house?"

He was giving her a lot of heavy things to consider. She pressed her lips together, not ready to say yes but not wanting to say no.

"I'll stay with you tonight, sand dragon. We can figure out all that serious stuff another time," Ocean said. He held out his hand to her. "Want to go to bed? And if you just want to sleep, I promise to be a gentleman."

Daisy took his hand, but she glanced at River. His status in the Triad made her want his permission. "Is this, okay?"

River grinned. "Goodnight to you both. There's no jealousy in the Triad, not really, not like if this was a human situation. I'll put away the perishables and we can get the rest in the morning. Rest well, both of you."

Ocean squeezed her hand. "My lady?"
Butterflies fluttered in her belly.

Chapter Three

Daisy let Ocean lead her out of the main house and down to the cottage. "Hang on," Ocean said as they went inside. The cottage was small. It didn't take him long to check all the rooms.

"Is it that likely Kai will come back?" Daisy's anxiety spiked.

"It's always better to be safe than sorry. Don't worry, you're safe on my watch." Ocean kicked his shoes off. "Are you sleepy?"

She was, but now that they were alone she couldn't help wondering what it would be like to sleep with just one of them. Would it be as amazing? Would it be weird with the others in the morning? "Not as much as I thought I would be. Are you really feeling better? Are you well enough for, umm… time alone?"

Ocean grinned. "I'm well enough for time alone with you, sand dragon." He wrapped his arms around her, brushing the hair out of her eyes. "And I'm happy to be holding you right now. This is the best medicine I can imagine." His kiss was slow and sweet as he claimed her lips, holding her close. She kissed him back, their lips dancing and her desire growing. When he broke the kiss, she brushed her lips across his chin.

Ocean watched as Daisy worked the buttons on his shirt free. Her pussy convulsed with the prickling excitement.

"You're mine tonight, sand dragon," Ocean whispered. There was a playfulness in his tone, but his manner couldn't hide the passion with which he made the declaration. When his lips came down to meet hers again, she melted into his arms. A fresh salt and sea scent infused the moment. She moaned against his lips. Nothing mattered but his kiss.

Daisy twined her tongue with his and wrapped her arms around his neck. The bond stirred something deep inside her. He pulled back to look at her. Daisy ran her hands up his biceps until they rested on the top of his shoulders. He gazed down at her, and she saw a spark of something she was uncomfortable putting a name to in his eyes.

Love. Sex and love weren't the same. She was in love with him and the whole Triad. It was crazy, but she loved them all. Through the bond, she felt it too. He was in love with her. She was in love with him -- all of them. And there was no saving her from this crazy, merman-filled life now.

Desire sent a wave of wet heat dampening her panties -- heat that crept up her neck to warm her checks. She couldn't remember ever being this turned on except for maybe the first night with them all.

He pulled her close again, cupping her lower back. She felt delicate in his grasp. He kissed her with a demanding savagery that stole her breath. She'd never responded so completely to a kiss. This was primal, hot. She wanted him -- bad. He growled low in his throat. Instead of scaring her, the sound intensified her response. Whimpering against his mouth, she pressed her body closer. Her pussy ached and convulsed. Emptiness. Shock caused her to gasp and pull back. The kiss was so much. She felt him through her entire body. His need fueled hers through the bond. She gazed up at him as the growing darkness of twilight crept into the room, his features fierce in the shadows.

"What are you doing to me?" she moaned. Arrows of desire prickled in her cunt and her breath became uneven panting. Something hard poked into her hip. Ocean was as affected as she was. The proof of his desire marveled her.

Ocean could have taken any woman in that bar home tonight. Her Triad were mythical, powerful beings, but they wanted her.

He pulled back. "You're my mate, sand dragon. There will never be another woman I want. Stop doubting yourself." He breathed the words raggedly against her cheek. Burning need scalded her soul as she clung to him. He kissed her throat, and she arched her back. "Mine."

She shivered and ran her fingers over his tight, muscular abs. His body delighted her senses. Ocean unzipped his fly and then worked his jeans off his hips before kicking them into the darkness.

A thin patch of wiry hair between his nipples trailed down to his belly button. His body was like her private amusement park where she didn't have to wait in line to ride. The ab muscles under her hands rippled. She traced the path. He growled, and she couldn't stop the quiet laugh that bubbled up.

"Am I funny looking without my clothes?" he teased.

"No. I'm just happy."

He kissed the top of her head. "So am I."

Ocean panted against her neck. She couldn't stop the fleeting moment of self-consciousness. He cupped her cheek with his palm. "Why do you look so serious?" he whispered.

"Because you're amazing and magical. I'm just a boring human. I'm waiting for you all to figure that out."

"You're perfect," he insisted, tilting her face up to look at him. "You're everything I've ever wanted. Long ago, my world was a very gloomy place. I couldn't even imagine the light. You're like a thousand suns burning away that darkness." He brushed her lower lip with the pad of his thumb.

Daisy closed her eyes and inhaled his scent. "Is this really happening?"

"Hell yes," he replied in a tone strained with need. "You're overdressed." Ocean pulled her tank top over her head. Then he pushed her shorts off her hips before looping his fingers in her lace panties. With a yank he ripped them from her body. "I'll buy you a new pair," he muttered.

She moaned, the violence of his passion making her hotter. He sucked one nipple through the lace of her bra, then cupped her ass cheeks and switched nipples. Ocean unhooked the bra with a few quick tugs and the fabric floated down to join the rest of her clothing. He used the pads of his thumbs to brush her tits as he took her breasts in his hands, stroking until she groaned and arched into his touch, then skimmed her ribs before rubbing his palms against her back. He pulled her close, his erection pressing against her belly.

Daisy reached out and took his thick cock in her hand. He was hard, and the velvet sensation of his skin in her palm was silken steel. She stroked him in a slow rhythm that pulled a moan from deep in his chest.

Grinning, she relished her power as she watched his eyes darken with lust. Ocean savaged her mouth with his. Images of him pumping into her with animalistic passion played like a porno in her brain. She moaned into his mouth as he controlled the kiss. His fingers tangled in her loose hair as he clutched her head to his.

Daisy trailed her hand down his shoulder and chest until she traced the defined muscles of his abdomen. He brought his mouth to her breast, and he kissed her nipple reverently before drawing it into his mouth and sucking hard.

She continued stroking the length of his cock, tightening her grip with careful precision. He sucked in a breath and let it out with a groan that was almost a sigh. She explored the silken steel of him. Pleasure made her shiver as he ran his teeth over her nipple. She closed her eyes and rubbed her hand faster up and down his cock.

He moved to devour her other nipple. He sucked, then released before nibbling her clit in a rhythmic pattern that forced a long moan and a sigh of pleasure from her.

When she cupped his sac, he sucked in a quick breath. "We should move this to the bedroom." His breath blew ragged against her ear before he kissed her neck. "I don't want to fuck you. I want to make love to you."

"I want you right here and right now. I need you," she confessed.

Daisy gasped in surprise as Ocean picked her up. "You'll have me soon enough. But I'm not taking you on the table." Ocean chuckled.

Daisy nodded fiercely and bit her lip. "Anywhere you want. Anything you want."

When they got to the bedroom, he laid her down on the mattress and crouched over her without breaking eye contact, his movements endearingly careful.

She reached up to rub his stubble-rough cheek because she didn't know what to do with the emotions bubbling up inside her heart and she needed to touch him.

He leaned on his arm and looked down at the beautiful pussy between her legs. "I can smell how much you want me."

She didn't resist as he parted her thighs and dropped a kiss just under her navel before his head dipped between her legs. His rough tongue slowly laved her clit. The sensation made her hips jerk. He clasped onto her sides, and he held her still as his strokes became a rapid assault of sensation. Daisy closed her eyes and let her body respond to him in a mindless joy. A rivulet of moisture ran down her ass and she wasn't sure if it was his saliva or her response to him, but she squirmed. Ocean held her firmly.

"You're mine. Hold still, sand dragon. I'm not done enjoying you yet."

"Ocean," she cried. "More."

He worshiped her with his tongue, each stroke pushing her further than she'd ever gone before. She shattered against his mouth and the whimpers turned into cries. She turned her head to the side and pressed the back of her hand against her mouth to stop the escalating volume.

"Let it out." He paused his ministrations. "The only people who could hear would love your screams. Say my name, sand dragon. Tell me what you want."

"Ocean! Fuck me. Please, I -- I need you. I want you to --" She cried out as he pinched her nipple, hard. "More!" Groaning, she ground herself toward his mouth as he put it back on her pussy. Her hands tangled in his silky hair. Daisy reveled in the tumultuous gratification of orgasm. Her pussy clenched and she bucked. The sensation felt so good his passionate attention almost hurt as he kept going with relentless vigor. When she thought she couldn't take another second Ocean let her go.

She was still panting as he rolled her on top of him. He took both her breasts into his hands and rolled her nipples gently between his thumb and fingers while gazing up at her face. Instead of quenching her need, the orgasm only wetted her hunger for more of him. She wanted his cock. She moved so that her pussy hovered over his dick. She'd never been on top of a man like this before.

His eyes glowed brighter as she lowered herself onto him. She slowly worked herself onto his length and he groaned as she began to ride him. His left hand stayed at her breast, but his right hand snaked down to find her clit. He rubbed the pleasure point as her tight heat slid over him. Daisy moved, faster he rubbed her harder.

Ocean's hips match the rhythm she set as he thrust deeply inside her core. They fucked with hedonistic perfection and when she came this time, it was so blindingly intense she sobbed his name like a prayer. "Ocean!"

He rolled her off him and she found herself on her hands and knees. He thrust his cock back inside of her and to her delight, her pleasure rekindled. He held her hips and claimed her roughly. Every thrust hit her at the perfect angle. His body fit hers completely, and his stamina brought unshed tears to her eyes. "I'm so close."

He pumped into her harder. The joy built inside of her until another orgasm made her cry out. He wrapped her hair around his hand and pulled her head back. He kissed her neck and she wailed with the force of her release.

Ocean jerked and groaned her name with a tender devotion. His mouth remained pressed to her throat as her muscles gripped his cock, milking the last of his pleasure. Ocean pulled her into his arms and they both collapsed on the mattress, exhausted. One of his big hands caressed her shoulder and the side of her neck.

"Our souls needed this as much as our bodies did." He paused, giving her another crazy intense look. "Every time you make love to one of us, the bond grows for all of us."

"It -- everything felt right. I just hope no one is jealous tomorrow."

Ocean chuckled. "This need between us is more powerful than love and it's real. It's not lust. You're my mate -- our mate. There's nothing a human can compare it to. Your body -- your soul -- recognizes that you belong to me, but also that I am part of something greater than one. You aren't loving just me. It's simple, even when it's complicated. The others will have nights like this too. They felt what we enjoyed in a way a human couldn't understand. Don't worry. They're as happy as I am right now. Close your eyes and feel them through the bond."

Daisy closed her eyes. He was right. The invisible threads that connected them seemed to hum with a peace and joy that made her throat tighten with emotion. Daisy fell asleep in Ocean's arms, but it wasn't just his comfort she enjoyed. The love of her Triad blanketed her in warmth. They were all with her. And she would be with them on their odyssey to do the TV show thing and keep her men relevant in the world of programming.

* * *

Ocean brushed his lips across Daisy's forehead. Her nose wrinkled adorably. Watching her sleep was an interesting challenge. He enjoyed getting to know her expressions, but each time she sighed or moved he longed to wake her. Every moment that she was his and his alone felt precious.

He knew this peace couldn't last. Today was going to be a busy day and they could be walking -- or sailing, more accurately -- into danger. He wasn't ready to give up these precious moments of perfect peace just yet.

Ocean sensed River and Bayou as the door to the cabin opened. He pulled Daisy against him, and she snuggled into his warmth. River carried a tray and Bayou set a bag down on the chair across the room. River put the tray on the dresser before going over to Daisy's side of the bed and kneeling down. He rubbed her back, making her stretch. There was a lot to do today, so Ocean ignored his cock stirring to life as his mate began to rouse.

"Good morning." River moved to sit on the bed next to Daisy.

She rolled over, opening her eyes. "You're not Ocean," she said in a sleepy yet somehow playful tone.

"I'm glad you can tell us apart," River teased. He leaned over her, kissing her tenderly.

Bayou brought the tray over to the bed and sat down by her feet. "Coffee?"

"Yes, please. A girl could get used to this." Daisy sat up, bringing the sheet with her to cover her bare breasts.

A flash of lust rippled through the bond, but Daisy didn't seem to notice. Bayou handed Daisy and Ocean each a cup. Ocean grabbed a croissant off the tray that Bayou placed on next to Daisy's legs. River took a cup too. Bayou never drank coffee.

After a few sips of piping hot coffee, River reached out and took Daisy's free hand. "Today is going to be rough. We're taking the *Explorer* out to a spot between Florida and Bermuda to survey the site of a wreck. It borders an area in the Atlantic under

Aegean control." River took another sip from his cup. "And we'd like you to come with us."

"I don't want to be on your TV show," Daisy protested.

"We won't put you to work," Bayou said. "We just need to know you're safe. Kai won't try anything with the cameras around."

Daisy rubbed her eyes. "Are you sure? He could drag me off the boat and into the Bermuda Triangle or something." She yawned.

Bayou chuckled. "Don't worry. We're the ones dragging you to the triangle, but no one will drag you off the boat."

"Huh?" Daisy widened her eyes. "The Bermuda Triangle, for real?"

River glared at Bayou. "Don't let him scare you. This wreck is honestly in the Bermuda Triangle, but the only reason that area has a reputation for danger is the Aegeans. They're the ones causing boats and planes to sink in that spot. You'll be safe with us. They have dark technology from the ancient days that humans have forgotten."

Daisy turned her attention to him. "Ocean, did you know the plan last night?"

He focused on his breakfast instead of looking at her. "Yeah."

"Why didn't you say anything?"

Ocean huffed out a sigh. "It had been a long day. I figured it could wait until morning. I just didn't realize we'd be talking about it this early. I wasn't trying to keep anything from you."

Daisy plucked a croissant off the tray and took a bite, but she was still scowling at him.

"Are you afraid?" Ocean asked. "We won't force you to go, but you know we won't let anyone hurt you.

These dives can take several days to film. A full exploration can take months. And with everything going on, the truce we'd had with Kai's kingdom is currently questionable. We honestly don't know how his legionnaires will react. But he'll know we're there. Even with your new vocal talent, we thought having you with us would be safest."

Daisy swallowed the bite she was chewing. "What if I get seasick or freak out? I've never been on a boat except for those couple rides to and from the island."

"We'll be there for you," River said. "The bond we share should help any physical reactions and if you start to get nervous, we'll know that, too. There's a bag of stuff I picked up for you. Warm hats and waterproof outerwear. There's a couple of packages of thermals for you to layer under your clothing. This isn't the optimal time of year for a dive, so we're only doing enough to set things up for the next season of our show. We just need to get the initial dives and on-the-boat interview footage for this season. We've got a team that works with us for the production."

"If you guys think I can handle it, I guess I can give this a try. How many days will we be gone?"

"Three," River said. "And if you're lucky we'll get just enough of you in a clip to thrill Sally without making you part of the show."

Daisy chuckled. "She would get awfully excited to see me on TV."

"If you're unlucky or lippy, we'll make you swab the deck," Bayou mumbled.

Daisy tossed the remainder of her croissant at him. The pastry hit him between the eyes. River and Ocean both laughed. Even Bayou's lips twitched in a quick smile.

Ocean reached out and ran his hand soothingly over Daisy's arm, pushing his love for her into *gift*. He wondered if the worry rippling through the bond was hers or theirs.

* * *

Daisy watched the waves break against *The Explorer*. She'd never thought about what went into their work until now. There was so much going on. River stood a few feet away, giving brief instructions to the cameraman. "At these depths we'll only have about thirty minutes to explore the wreck. If this wreck is the *SS Aphrodite*, we might have uncovered one of the biggest lost hauls of gold and silver we've ever discovered. The ship was lost in 1920 with all 96 of her crew. Today, we'll see if she's been found and if her treasure trove is still down there waiting."

The cameraman gave River the thumbs up before gathering his gear. Bayou carried a large tank as he walked past her. River rushed over to him. "Make sure the heaters are working and all the tanks for the camera crew are triple checked."

Grunting, Bayou nodded as he continued on his way.

"Can I do anything to help?" Daisy asked, feeling like dead weight.

"Nope," River replied. "Just stay safe. If you're cold, you can go to my cabin. We're diving in about twenty minutes."

Daisy nodded.

River turned and scowled. "I've got to deal with this. Hey, don't --" and then he was rushing off toward two men and a pile of equipment.

Daisy gazed out into the vast ocean. If someone had told her two weeks ago she'd be standing in the middle of the Bermuda Triangle, she'd have said they were insane. But here she was. Ocean stopped behind her and put his hands on her shoulders, then ran his palms down her arms. That wonderful worry-free feeling he always gave her stole the tingle of apprehension from her mind.

"Shouldn't you be saving your strength?" Daisy chided. "You don't know what's down there -- or who might be waiting. I'm fine."

"Can't a man touch his beautiful mate?" Ocean whispered in her ear.

"Not right before he does something dangerous," Daisy retorted. "Promise me all three of you will come back safe and sound."

"Scout's honor. Besides, River's doing the diving today."

Daisy chuckled. "Merpeople have Boy Scouts?"

"No, but if we did, I'd have been the best one." Ocean straightened his back and his chin rose pridefully. Then his expression darkened. "We'll be fine as long as we know you're okay."

"I promise not to fall off the boat." Daisy turned to face him. They were so close she could have reached up to kiss him, but with all the crew around she held back.

"That's all we can ask," he replied with just a hint of sensuality in his voice. "I'm looking forward to how you're going to reward us for returning unharmed. Maybe a kiss?"

"If there weren't so many people on board I'd kiss you right now," she whispered.

"Someday, we'll figure out how to bring you to Atlantis. You can kiss all three of us in the middle of the city and no one would think it's odd. I don't like your human hang-ups about Triad."

Daisy scowled. "They aren't my hang-ups.

They're cultural. Women don't just date three guys openly on land, you know."

Ocean grinned. "You know what we have is more than frivolous dating. I want to kiss your cute little nose right now so badly it hurts."

"When we're alone, I'll smooch all your pain away." She wanted to kiss each of her guys thoroughly before they dove under the cold, dark water, but she knew that wasn't smart. The last thing any of them needed was tabloid attention. Three hunks and their maid on a private island would make any shutterbug excited if there was even a hint that she was more than just the help. They might not be A-list Hollywood famous, but any kind of notoriety attracted scandal and drew reporting vultures. "You'll just have to tough it out until we're home. Then I expect double kisses from all of you."

"Yes, ma'am." Ocean turned and looked toward the equipment. "Okay, looks like River needs me. Stay safe." He rushed off and she stood alone again.

She hadn't realized how upsetting being separated would be. When any of them dove she'd be helpless to follow them. She'd have the bond, but there was a discomfort in the distance. She'd noticed it the day they'd gone to town, but shrugged it off. Facing how connected they were had been easier to ignore than to truly consider the implications. Now there was no ignoring the reality. Even with experience there was danger in what they did. Her connection to them was a living, breathing thing that was so much bigger than she'd let herself accept. How had she let this happen? How had she gone from commitment-phobic to *this* in less than two weeks? She was glad they'd brought her along. If she'd be left on the island, she'd have gone crazy with worry by now.

The crew had a second ship anchored close. She watched the activity on the *Sunrise*. There were so many people and all of them were rushing here and there. She thought about going to River's cabin to warm up a few times, but each time she changed her mind. At least she could watch her guys working for now. She didn't want the odd sense of bereavement to start before it had to.

Daisy jumped as angry voices startled her and she turned around to see what was happening on *The Explorer*. One of the camera crew was arguing with one of the dive team. River rushed over. The diver balled his hands into a fist.

River stepped between the men. "Tensions are high. I get it. This is an important session. If we don't get the footage, we might have to delay next season's premier. We might even get canceled. But violence isn't going to solve anything." He straightened suddenly and put his fingers against his temples before collapsing.

Daisy gasped and rushed over to him. She shook him gently. "River?"

He blinked his eyes open. "G -- get the others. My… cabin."

Daisy nodded and stood. "He needs to lie down. Help him to his cabin," she ordered the men who'd been fighting. Then she dashed off to find Bayou and Ocean.

Chapter Four

River wondered if the others had heard Kai. It was clear Daisy hadn't, so the humans were unaware. That was good. The last thing they needed was Kai outing them. He allowed the human men to help him into his cabin on *The Explorer* and lay him down.

"Sorry about the fighting," muttered Tom, the dive team member.

"Yeah, you gonna be okay, dude?" asked the cameraman whose name River couldn't remember.

"I'll be okay, just need to rest," River lied.

The cabin door opened. Ocean, Daisy, and Bayou entered.

"We've got him," Bayou said. "Get back to work. We're staying on schedule."

The two men nodded and left.

Ocean sat down on the bed and began running his fingers over River's temples. "Dick move on Kai's part, sending that pitch into your head."

Bayou grunted. "I heard the threat, but not the pitch."

"Me too," Ocean said.

"What pitch? What threat?" Daisy's worried tone wasn't helping his head. When her voice rose just right her *gift* began. None of them had had the heart to say anything, but eventually they'd have to tell her.

Through the bond River felt her rising fear just as clearly as he felt Ocean and Bayou's anger.

"Kai has Aerwyna," River said between gritted teeth. "If we don't bring *you* to him, he's going to kill her."

"Me?" Daisy squeaked.

"We aren't bringing her to him," Bayou growled. "And watch how high you let your voice go! Damn it, woman."

"But Aerwyna --"

"No!" Bayou interrupted Daisy. "It's too damn dangerous."

Ocean nodded. "He's right. It's too risky."

Daisy scowled. "We have to do everything we can to save her. Do you have a plan?" she asked, sitting down on the bed next to River.

"I do, but I think it'll be a hard sell." River knew how he'd feel if one of the others suggested a similar idea.

Ocean's gaze narrowed. "Hard sell? You mean it involves using Daisy as bait?"

"No," Bayou growled as he sat next to Daisy.

"We'll bring Daisy with us," River looked up at Daisy. "You have to sing."

Her beautiful eyes grew wide. "Won't I hurt you guys too? Like karaoke?"

"No," River shook his head. "We'll be prepared for it, but Kai won't."

"What about Aerwyna?" Daisy frowned.

River smiled. "That's why this is perfect. Aerwyna's *gift* is that she's not affected by *gift*. Your voice won't bother her a bit. It's why she was never afraid around Bayou."

"Wow, yeah, that's perfect. I won't let that jerk hurt me. We're going to save Aerwyna and defeat Kai. And wait a second --" She turned her attention to Bayou. "You told me a little while ago to watch how high my voice goes. Does it hurt you guys when I talk?"

Bayou frowned. "Only if you get all excited, but we'll deal. Forget it. We have more immediate matters to deal with. Defeating Kai won't be easy. Not even close to easy. If he gets his filthy hands on you, we might not be able to get you back. I've been his prisoner. The thought of you in that position makes me crazy. Once he realizes you have an easily weaponized *gift*, he'll seek to use that to his advantage, or destroy you." His nostrils flared as he looked into her eyes. "I don't like this."

The corner of her lip quirked up. "I know. I can feel it. So, feel *me*. Feel how much I want to do this for Aerwyna."

Bayou remained quiet for a moment. Finally, he turned his hand so he could take hers in his and squeezed her fingers. "I don't want you to go, but I won't stop you. If we lose you, we lose everything. Don't you realize how much you mean to us?"

She shrugged. "I know. But I couldn't live with myself if we don't try."

"Then we'll try." Bayou stood. He paced next to the bed. His agitation saturated the bond. He stopped, gazing into Daisy's eyes intently. "I won't stop you, but I don't accept this. I don't want to lose you."

Ocean sat down next to her and ran his fingers over her arm. "Don't feel guilty. This isn't your fight."

Daisy jerked her arm away. "Don't use your *gift* to dissuade me. That's -- that's a violation."

Ocean held his hands up. "I can take away your worry." He glared at River. "Kai might not even have Aerwyna. He could be lying."

"But if he does," Daisy argued, "we can't let her die."

"But we can risk your life?" Bayou's brow rose and his jaw was set. "No."

Daisy stood, suddenly toe-to-toe with Bayou. "You don't have a choice. I'm doing this."

Rage filled Bayou's expression. River had never seen such a darkness cloud his friend's eyes. Daisy gave a small gasp.

Bayou flinched. "I would never hurt you. Never!" Bayou said between gritted teeth. "I can handle everyone else in the sea or above it being afraid of me, but never you." He turned and stormed out of the cabin.

Daisy turned back, glancing between River and Ocean. "I want to do this."

"I know," River's throat tightened with gratitude. "We won't stop you or let Kai touch you."

Ocean sighed as he stood up. "I'm going to join Bayou. I think he'll need a little bit of *gift*."

"Just make sure he really wants your help. Don't push him." Daisy turned her attention away from Ocean and back to River. "We need to figure out this plan. Everything depends on getting this right."

River nodded. Daisy's love flowed through the bond. He hoped his strategy wouldn't doom them all.

* * *

River motioned for the crew. He hated putting the livelihoods of these good people in jeopardy, but he had to get the humans away from his Triad. This five-day shoot had to end now. He watched as the underwater crew set up the first scenes for the dive.

If he could break the gravimeter and the main lights, and make it look like an accident, the production would end. The humans would be forced to return to shore. It was expensive and dark. If he just walked away, they couldn't film, but that would leave everyone with questions. He didn't want to cause suspicions that would lead to discovery. Protecting the Triad and Daisy were all that mattered. Even if he destroyed what they'd built for themselves in the human world.

This meant the next season would be delayed, and they'd face the chance of cancellation, but he couldn't worry about that now. Daisy and his sister were all that mattered. The last thing any of them needed was a camera crew catching a mer on video.

He had to get them away without making it obvious. Bayou would already have demolished the equipment like a wrecking ball if it were up to him. River preferred subtlety. Ocean had admitted he liked both of their ideas. River honestly wondered if Ocean was leaning more toward Bayou's chaos.

If River didn't feel responsible for forming the Triad, he would've been ready to give in to chaos too. He needed to protect their freedom to live with the humans. This life gave them something they'd lose in Atlantis. River would always be a prince, but they'd always be considered traitors. On land, they could be themselves -- themselves with a secret.

Would any of them ever really be free? The idea of Kai putting his scaly hands on Daisy made River homicidal, but if he did this right, both his sister and their mate would be safe. And the life they'd built could continue.

River was with some of the more experienced team members. They swam through the deep azure water. The silt stirred a bit, but they still managed to get good video. He took note of the camera angles. Making this look like an accident wasn't going to be easy. He swam down to where they'd planned the initial exploration. He knew exactly where the treasure was and how to extend the drama of finding it. They could splice in some of the videos from earlier in the season too. There was a lot of opportunity to make this exciting.

But right now, he needed to position the team where he could collapse the upper deck on himself without hurting his divers. He could crush the sensitive equipment with his mer-strength, and the humans would believe it was bad luck and a mistake on his part.

All these ideas swirled in his head as he swam. But he'd have to take action soon. He could feel Daisy's concern through the bond. He hated putting her through this too. If there was any way to just call off the dive, he'd do it, but that wasn't possible.

Swimming into the hole in the side of the ship, he made a strategic decision to lead them left. They'd still be able to film next season if the collapse happened as he imagined it would. This would look dramatic, and maybe they could salvage things with the right spin.

He swam past a grouper fish and pointed to where coral was growing below them. They were close enough to the exit that his human team should be able to escape. River uncharacteristically motioned for the main light. It took a moment for the diver to give in and let River direct the angle. He subtly wrapped the cable around his arm as he positioned it down a hole leading to a lower deck.

Below, a small sand tiger made for a beautiful shot and while the crew's attention was on the predator, River used his inhuman grip to loosen the plank just over his head. He felt the weight of the decomposing wood above him give and it was time.

River thrashed enough to capture the crew's attention a moment before letting go. Relief washed through him as the others dodged the danger. He let the collapse take him down, yanking the light with him. It was over in a moment. He wished he could transform, but that would be too risky. Instead, he forced himself to remain in his land-form as he avoided the most dangerous debris. He just needed this to look real. The drama of a mistake could sell. The proof he wanted to end the shoot would equal questions.

Protecting those he loved was more valuable than any equipment or even the show. It killed him inside to be so willing to give up everything they'd built. But losing his mate or Triad was unacceptable.

His strong mer body didn't break under the impact as the wreckage made contact. If he'd been a normal human, he'd be dead. Pain hit him from every angle as he sank.

Grunting, he closed his eyes. Through the bond, he experienced the moment the others felt his pain. Terror and sadness coursed through the invisible threads that tied their souls together. Then there was a moment where they realized they were going to die with him, and it caused him to struggle harder. The lights were completely out. Even with his mer eyesight, all he could see was pieces of the ship as it carried him to the lower decks. He prayed to the gods he hadn't miscalculated.

Was he strong enough? He had to be strong enough. Everyone he loved depended on him.

A large piece of iron was coming right at his face.

* * *

Pleasure coursed through River. Was this an amazing dream? Blinking his eyes open, he groaned as he glanced down. Daisy sucked his cock. She looked so beautiful with her mouth full of him. Her hair cascaded over his hip. He grinned. As good as it felt, he wanted to kiss her. River lurched and had her on her back. She gave a single, surprised squeak and glared up at him. He laughed.

River pulled her into his lap. He was hard and ready for his mate. Brushing his lips against hers she moaned. The sound was music to his ears. He deepened the kiss.

She pulled away. "I want to take care of you, always. Being yours makes me whole in a way I've never been. I've been working on cooking things suited to your Atlantean palate. The first thing I'm going to do is feed you."

"I want to eat, but it's pussy I'm hungry for," he whispered in her ear.

Daisy shivered. "I think that might be on the menu."

River pulled her to him again, kissing her hard. Every ounce of love he felt for her he pushed into that kiss. He groaned. "I could do with a helping," he said in a strained tone. "My cock has missed you, but it's my heart that's hungry."

This time she kissed him. He grinned against her mouth. Their tongues touched in an erotic dance. Daisy tore her mouth off his. "I want you to fuck me," she said in a quiet, soft voice.

"Your wish is my command." His smile slipped as he saw tears slip down her cheeks.

"I love you so much. When you died, it was so awful. I had to watch as the others die and then I died too. Dying hurt, River. It hurt so much."

River sat up. "What?" His heart raced. He tried to remember where he was. "Daisy?" She appeared so pale. "Gods no, I'm not dead."

"You will be if you don't wake up," she whispered. "Wake up, River, please."

* * *

Awakening, River bucked, pinned, trapped under the weight of rotting wood. His vision blurred again and narrowed to a pinpoint, but he forced himself not to give in. He heard static in the com he wore in his ear. Through the bond, he sensed the hysteria of the others. They were desperate for word. Desperate to help. He hoped they could feel his life and that Ocean and Bayou wouldn't do anything stupid, like go full-on merman in front of a human camera crew. He pushed his love for Daisy toward them.

He shoved a thick beam that held him trapped off his chest. A human would never have been able to do that. He had to be sure none of the rescuers saw him. He did what he could to shift the carnage off his body, without making his miracle survival too obvious.

A light shone down through a hole above him. He waved an arm and waited for the crew to free him. He tried to send thoughts of calm to his Triad and mate, but his head was still fuzzy from the hit he'd taken. He fought for consciousness but was losing. If they didn't get to him soon, he'd be at the mercy of the deep.

* * *

Daisy held her breath as she watched the dive team hoist River out of the water. "He's alive, I feel it," she whispered to Ocean.

Ocean took her hand and squeezed. "River's smart. Strong. He'll pull through."

She wished Ocean sounded more certain. She wondered if he was trying to assure her or himself. Her connection to River seemed to grow weaker by the second. "Will --" Her voice cracked. "Will strength be enough?"

Ocean wrapped his arm around her shoulder.

Bayou came rushing up to the railing, skidded,

and changed direction. He normally wouldn't have gotten this close to any of the human crew, but he grabbed the edge of the backboard they had River strapped to and helped them get River onboard. He stepped away from one of the divers who got too close so fast that he fell backward.

Bereavement hit Daisy as Ocean let go of her and hurried over to River. A lump rose in her throat as tears threatened to fall. She watched River grab Ocean's arm and grip it tight. Something unspoken passed between them. The ripple of it hit her as it rolled through the Triad bond.

Bayou glanced to her. She knew he felt the moment too.

Ocean stood up. "We need to get him to a hospital."

Terror gripped Daisy. A hospital? His injuries must be worse than she'd thought. His body wasn't human, and she couldn't imagine that he'd want a human doctor finding out what he was.

Ocean motioned to one of the dinghies. "We'll take him. Turn off the cameras. Only family, and that includes Daisy. We'll be faster in that."

"Sir," said one of the crew. "Should we radio for a helicopter?"

"No. This is the fastest way. We'll be in touch. But with the weather and his injuries, we have to postpone until the seasons change." A general grumble rose from several of the crew. Ocean scowled in the direction of the discontent. "We'll figure the show out. His life means more than renewal. Let's go." Ocean turned to Bayou. "You know what to do."

Bayou rushed below deck. Daisy just stood helplessly. Uncertainty left her anxious and pacing. Ocean glanced at her. "This is the best way." She still had no idea what that meant.

Bayou came back up from the cabin with a couple of bags.

"Return to port," Ocean ordered. "We'll get him the help he needs."

There was a flurry of activity. Daisy wrapped her arms around herself. Before she knew what was happening Bayou was ushering her into the smaller boat. Ocean tossed a few duffle bags into the boat before he climbed in beside her. "It'll be okay," he whispered.

She didn't think any of this was okay, but she nodded. Once there were all on the small vessel with River's prone body wrapped up in blankets, Bayou handed her a life jacket which she quickly and gratefully put on. The craft was lowered into the cold, angry water. They bounced against the waves as Ocean started up the engine and sped away from the larger boat.

River lay still, his eyes closed. Daisy desperately wanted to touch him, kiss him, comfort him. Nothing in her life had prepared her for such intense feelings. They were out of earshot when Ocean looked up and grinned. "He'll be fine. But we can't have the crew see Kai. It's on. There's nothing we can do except fight. The humans need to go back to port. Our show is fucked, but River has done what he can to protect the Triad."

"What do you mean?" Daisy's tone was sharper than she'd expected.

"River risked his life to get us out of there. He's healing, but he needs rest. By the time we arrive to confront Kai he'll be good."

Bayou grunted.

Daisy scoffed. "He put us through that for

appearances?"

River opened his eyes. "Daisy --"

Ocean put his hand on River's shoulder. "Don't worry, I'll smooth this over."

"Smooth it over? Do you mean with me or the crew?" Daisy's brow rose. "I doubt I'll ever forgive any of you if you knew this was the plan and didn't tell me. River, if you weren't hurt, I'd kill you myself. Never. Ever! Do something that stupid again. There had to be a better way to get the boat back to shore without almost dying."

Tears clouded her vision. She wouldn't apologize for crying. How selfish could he be?

Ocean reached for her, but she flinched back and away from his touch. "Don't!" She shook her head. "Don't use *gift* on me. This is unreal. Why would he put us through this for the sake of a stupid TV show?"

Bayou chuckled. "It's actually a pretty popular show."

When Daisy glared at him, Bayou put up his hands.

Daisy wiped her wet cheeks. "I don't care if it's the number one TV show in the world. What he did is unforgivable. What if he'd died?"

Bayou had the grace to look embarrassed. "He didn't die. He's our prince and the foundation of our Triad. I trust him with my life. If he'd died. I'd have died. But we're all here still alive. Now we must be strong for him like he was for us."

Daisy felt their disapproval through the bond. She sat back, quiet, but far from mollified. They turned once they were far enough away from the bigger vessel and human sight. "Where are we going?" she asked.

"To Kai," Ocean answered. "To save Aerwyna. He'll show. I'm not sure when, but he will come for us."

Daisy let that thought pass through her. "What should I sing?"

Bayou snorted. "Anything. You're not good."

Daisy glared while Ocean slugged him in the arm. "What he means," Ocean said softly, "is please sing something that will make you hit all the high notes."

Daisy was willing to do everything she could to support her guys. Honestly, she was mad and considered singing Bayou a special, soprano only, rendition of "Bodies" by Drowning Pool, but didn't want to kill her men for real. Even if they deserved it right now.

Chapter Five

By the time Ocean beached the boat on a small island that was little more than an uninhabited sandbar off the coast of the Florida Keys, River was sitting up. As relieved as Daisy felt to see him upright, her anxiety about the coming conflict was over-the-top. She nervously fingered the pendant Aerwyna had given her. Even if it was stolen from the woman's family jewels it was a connection to the friend she'd come to care for. River stayed with her in the boat while Ocean and Bayou got out to investigate. There were a few palm trees on the small patch of land, but otherwise the island appeared deserted.

Daisy didn't see any sign of Kai, his guards, or Aerwyna. Had they fallen into some kind of trap? She gazed out across the ocean. The sky overhead was cloudy. With her human eyesight she couldn't detect anything suspicious. Did the guys see anything she didn't? She couldn't feel any heightening concern when she reached out to them through the bond.

A loud splash to her right caught her attention. She turned, squinting against a single shaft of sunlight that found its way through the clouds. Tightness and pain hit her around her midsection. River cursed. Ocean lunged toward her and grabbed her hand. The force behind her was too strong and too heavy. She couldn't pull away and her fingers slipped through Ocean's. The world tilted. The sky above was so gray, but darkly beautiful as she tumbled backward. This was it. She would die. The cold water surrounded her, shocking her. And then -- she was submerged.

Water made her layers of clothing heavier. She

tried to pull herself up to the surface. Panic set in. The life jacket was no use against the inhuman strength holding her under the water. Struggling, she tried to free herself. She held her breath until her chest burned. In her panic she opened her eyes. The ocean was beautiful, and for an instant she was glad her last sight would be something unique and peaceful. She thrashed in Kai's grip. Finally, the oxygen deprivation became too much, and she couldn't stop a gasp.

Water didn't fill her lungs. The pendant hanging between her breasts glowed bright. Instead of dying, she breathed in the sea. Her neck hurt, and for a moment Kai's grip loosened. Daisy managed to push herself away from him and swim through the water to surface for a gasp of real air. The water had been as real as oxygen for the second she thought she'd breathed her last breath.

She sputtered "What the fuck?" as she dog-paddled toward the island. "River!" she screamed just as she was pulled under again.

"How are you alive?" rang in her head -- Kai. He spoke to her like she was a mer. Instinctively, she knew. And she didn't have the foggiest idea how it was possible, but she had the same powers as a mer. The pain... she touched her neck and felt gills sprouting out of her skin. She kicked out and her foot connected with Kai's abdomen. It wasn't like mermen in mer form had balls, so she'd aimed for his stomach. He grunted, and she used that moment to fight her way away. She couldn't swim, but she managed to pull her body through the water in the direction of the island. She moved faster and easier than she'd have thought possible. Each movement felt natural, right.

Miraculously, she bobbed to the surface. Bayou hauled her out of the water. Fear and confusion clouded his eyes and mirrored her own feelings. "I'm alive," she mumbled.

"Thank the gods," he replied as he wrapped his arms around her. "Thank the gods."

Ocean knelt in the sand beside her. "Are you okay?"

She nodded. "Kai?"

River was just about to dive into the water. Daisy noticed he held a spear gun.

"Don't!" Daisy cried. "He wants that. Don't go. I'm okay. Stay with me. He's leaving." The pendant around her neck was hot against her skin. She wasn't even sure how she felt it, but her slight connection to the enemy, as if she were of his kind, was stretching as he ran -- swam -- away.

"How was that possible?" Bayou asked.

Daisy looked down at her gifted necklace. "Aerwyna. She gave me this. Best gift ever." She pulled the necklace out of her shirt and held it up by the chain so that the pendant dangled in the air.

They all looked at the glowing sea glass. Through the bond she felt their excitement and fear. River was next to her. He took her face tenderly in his hands and kissed her as he knelt beside her. "I thought we'd lost you," he muttered when he pulled away.

"Not that lucky," she retorted.

"Not funny," said Bayou. "Losing you is losing everything."

She shrugged. "I live to fight another day. Remind me to thank Aerwyna when we save her. Where do you think Kai will go?"

"Good question," Ocean said as he stood to survey the ocean stretching out past the boat. "That's a very good question."

"River?" Daisy asked. "What do you know about

this necklace?"

River knelt next to her and took a long look at the pendant. "Aerwyna has more forethought than I've ever given her credit for. She was always more interested in the history of our people than I was. She really should have been born Father's heir."

Daisy frowned. "What do you mean?"

"The pendant saved your life. When you go into the water wearing this, you become mer."

"Mer?" Daisy squeaked, then quickly slapped a hand over her mouth, looking up at Bayou apologetically. "Sorry. Trying to remember not to get pitch-y with you. I can't swim. Wearing this, the water wasn't as scary as it should have been. I felt like I could move, and I think I had... gills?"

River expression grew stern. "You'll be able to swim with a little more practice. This will allow you to breathe under the water. Don't take it off. Promise me."

Daisy nodded. "I promise I won't take this necklace off."

Ocean went to the boat and opened one of the duffel bags. He brought Daisy a change of clothes. "Let's get you dry."

There was no one around but her men, so she stripped off the wet clothing and brushed at the sand sticking to her damp skin as she dressed in the fresh clothing. It was chilly, but at least they were in a naturally warm climate. She'd have died of exposure if this had happened in waters closer to home. She touched the necklace again. "Will I be able to sing under the water? Did I lose my chance to kill Kai?"

River's brow furrowed. "I'm not sure about singing under water. Mer use telepathy in the water. When we're under the domes of Atlantis we speak out loud. In any case, your ability to survive under water is another tool we have to fight Kai. You'd have died without this piece of old magic. Remind me to thank my sister when we rescue her -- and to beg her to forgive me for teasing her for all the time she spent in the great library under the dome."

Bayou's expression stayed grim. "We owe her everything."

"I never imagined I'd be able to show you the kingdom I'll inherit." He glanced at Bayou and Ocean. "Our kingdom. It's so deep a human diver would die, but with this you'll be able to get there. The cold won't have as much effect on you, either. We have a chance now. I imagined Kai would confront us on land because he knows you're human. I wonder why he wants to trade for Aerwyna?"

"I've been suspicious ever since he sent you that message," Bayou grumbled. "We should take Daisy back to land and hide her in a motel somewhere. He's trying to take this battle under the water. He must have a reason to want Daisy. Now that he knows she can breathe under water I feel like she's not any safer than before. What if he takes the necklace from her?"

River shrugged. "If my memory serves me, he won't be able to get it off of her. She was given that by a blood relative of the first king of Atlantis. It's a free pass to come and go in our kingdom. In fact, my father can't even order her death, if the legend is correct. I'd forgotten all about it. I love my sister so dearly at this moment."

"This is very sweet," Ocean said. "But shouldn't we focus on Kai?"

Daisy shrugged. "We should. I say we fight that bastard with everything we have."

River chuckled. "You're our best defense. You

and your pitch."

Daisy frowned. "So, is it my choice of song or some note?"

"The higher the note you sing, the better. Or you could just do that squeaky thing." Bayou said.

River glared at him.

Daisy stuck her tongue out at Bayou. She did have a song in mind. "Okay, I'll call on my inner Sally and rock some acapella. We'll kick his mer ass! I just hope my pitch thing works under water."

"That's the spirit," Ocean quipped.

"You haven't even heard the song," Daisy replied.

"Nor do I plan to," he said. "Just make it a high note."

Daisy's narrowed her eyes. "Shouldn't I practice?"

"No!" all three said in unison.

She growled.

Bayou chucked. River and Ocean just gave her pensive glances.

"I just have a very unique voice," Daisy grumbled. There were lots of bad singers at karaoke. She knew she wasn't the worst. Maybe, second or third worst, but these three were giving her a complex. "I guess it'll be a girl's night from now on when I get together with Sally for karaoke. And I'm going to accept that I have a powerful voice." Her chin rose. "This is me staking my claim on being an autonomous human that's not defined or controlled by the man or *men* she sleeps with!"

River rolled his eyes, Ocean chuckled, and Bayou's gaze burned with sexy challenge. "Good to know. We'll see how long that lasts. We'll have you begging to be defined by what we do to you in bed."

Daisy crossed her arms over her chest. "Is now really the time for that?"

Ocean stepped between them. "We're not showing off our dicks here, right?"

Daisy rolled her eyes. "Since I don't have one, I guess not."

Bayou laughed. "You have three. You win. And just so you know, there's always time for *that*."

Daisy shrugged. "Don't try to be cute!"

"Never said I was," Bayou grumbled.

She shook her head. "You're cute. Right now, we need to figure out what Kai is trying to do and where he's holding Aerwyna."

Bayou grinned. "You're right, ignore how cute I am, focus."

"Okay," River said. "Our plan might need a little work, but we'll get my sister back."

Daisy nodded. "Great. What's the plan?"

"I'd love to know too," Ocean said.

"So would I." River sighed. "I thought we'd show up and Kai would be waiting for us with my sister. Daisy would sing. We'd use the ear protection. We'd get my sister away from him and leave here in victory. Now I have no idea what his game is."

"It's our turn to send him a message," Daisy said.

Her Triad just stared at her.

She rolled her eyes. "Come on, he sent River a telepathic message. Now we send him one."

"You make that sound a lot easier than it is." Ocean took her hand. "There is a lot of energy involved in long distance mer telepathy. It's much harder if you're reaching out to an enemy or stranger than it would a friend. It takes something a little dark to push a threat into another. What Kai did to River just proves how dangerous he is."

"I'll do it," Bayou said. "I'm the only one of us with that kind of angry energy."

Ocean put his hand on Bayou's arm. "And a push like that will hurt you almost as much as it hurts him. I won't let you."

Bayou jerked his arm away. "You don't have a choice." He stood up and walked a short distance. Daisy took a step toward him, and Bayou held out his hand. "Don't come any closer." He looked at Ocean. "If this is too much for her, protect her from me."

Ocean nodded.

Daisy didn't have a good feeling about what was happening.

Bayou closed his eyes and his fists clenched at his sides.

Daisy felt a blast of anger rippling through the bond. Intense emotions hit her and swirled inside of her. She dropped to her knees. Ocean was beside her, and she felt his *gift* touch her as the darkness growing in the bond engulfed them all. Everything good seemed to evaporate. There was nothing but hate and anger now. Everything in her soul hurt. All the energy drained from her as despair overwhelmed her. She put her face into Ocean's shoulder looking for protection and comfort, but there was nothing but the worst emotions. Nothing but bad.

And then it was over. Daisy collapsed into Ocean's arms.

Bayou was suddenly there beside her. "I'm sorry. I'm so sorry. I had to draw on your *gift* to magnify mine because yours -- yours is dark too."

She nodded, confused by all of it. How could he hurt her like that without warning her? She'd have helped. If she'd been prepared it wouldn't have been so bad, maybe. When she managed the courage to look at him, his expression was full of misery.

He touched her arm and she pulled away. "Just - - give me a moment."

He nodded and stood. She didn't watch him walk away. Ocean was doing his best to soothe her, but it felt like too little too late.

"He'll come," Bayou muttered from where he stood. "He'll come because I sent him all that my *gift* can do short of destroying his mind permanently."

* * *

Daisy wanted to talk to Bayou about what had happened, but she didn't know how. What could she say or ask to help her understand what had happened? Did he feel those terrible emotions all the time? If so, how did he function?

River had started a small bonfire and they were eating the snack bars and dried seaweed from one of the duffle bags Ocean brought. She'd noticed some weapons too. How bad would this be before they got Aerwyna back?

"How long do you think we'll have to wait?" Daisy asked.

A sound caught her attention. In the evening light, she noticed a ripple in the water. Through the bond, she experienced her Triad's anxiety spike.

Followed by his entourage, Kai walked out of the water with his chest puffed out and his chin jutting up. She wondered how long he'd practiced that scowl in a mirror. He wore an *I'm-better-than-you* smirk and nothing else. She was going to have to get used to the mer lack of modesty. The group strode up the beach with water streaming off them, seemingly unconcerned with her Triad.

"Give me your witch!" Kai demanded.

It took Daisy a second to realize she was the

witch in question. "I can't make your dick bigger," she declared boldly. "I guess my witchy powers are no use to you. Give us Aerwyna!"

Only Bayou chuckled. She glanced at him with a grateful grin.

River glared at Kai. "Where is my sister?"

"Safe. Alive," Kai said.

"Prove it."

Kai grinned. He held up a conch shell. An image of Aerwyna appeared. She was tied to a large coral chair. She was in human form and dressed only in a long tunic style top, but it preserved her modesty. Daisy wanted to punch the satisfied smile off Kai's evil face.

"Let her go!" River demanded.

Kai threw his head went back as he laughed. "I'm not a fool. Aerwyna is mine. She's promised to me. She is to be my wife."

Daisy realized Kai had spoken Atlantean and she had understood.

"Aerwyna hates you," River said.

"Arranged marriages." Kai waved his hand in the air. "They're not what anyone expects. But I could be happy with your beautiful sister."

Daisy had heard enough. "*You* could be happy? How the hell does Aerwyna feel about that? I very much doubt she'd consider you her Prince Charming after what you've put her through!"

Kai glared at Daisy. "Women are pretty adornments. Females are not meant to be heard from. What is wrong with your Triad that they let you speak out of turn? It's interesting that you've managed to teach your witch your tongue. I think I shall cut it from her mouth."

Daisy grimaced. "I speak when I want to speak.

I'm seen when I want to be seen. I'm heard when I want to be heard. You're a nightmare." She wanted to sing, but would she hurt her Triad? "I sing when I sing." She opened her mouth to start, but Bayou stepped between her and Kai.

Bayou crossed his arms over his chest. "We love her. We trust her. She completes us. That. Is. What. Triad. Means!"

Daisy wanted to clap.

Ocean nodded. "It's sad that a woman's strength scares you, Kai. Aerwyna is too much of a woman for you. Let her go and we'll find you a female who's easily impressed by your ego -- and nearsighted."

"Enough!" Kai roared.

Through the shell, they watched as another guard hit Aerwyna. She looked a little dazed. Her bravado clearly slipped as tears sprang to her eyes.

Daisy fought her urge to scream at Kai and demand Aerwyna's location. She felt River's anguish through the bond.

Kai closed his eyes. An energy seemed to ripple from him across the island and over the water. In the projection on the shell, Daisy watched the guards around Aerwyna stumble. They glanced at each other. One of them pulled out what appeared to be a huge sword and pointed it at Aerwyna's chest.

"Stop!" River roared.

"Okay," Daisy said, putting up her hand toward Kai mollifying. "Okay, sure, she's not some sweet, pliable princess, but she's strong. Would you honestly want a girl you could manipulate? Don't hurt her. If she's your future mate, please don't do this."

Kai paused. "My mate, my truest mate, will be a warrioress."

Daisy smiled. She had his attention. "Exactly. No

one in the world above or under the sea would see Aerwyna as anything else. Just let her go. If she's really meant for you, she will be with you."

"Don't try to trick me, feeble human!" Kai spat.

"I'm not," Daisy protested. She meant it. "If our Aerwyna is the mate for you, she knows it as well."

Kai glared. "I don't need some human telling me about being mer!"

Daisy shrugged. "I don't need some mer telling me about love. I feel it for my Triad."

They glared at each other until Kai tipped his head back and laughed. "Spirited." He narrowed his eyes menacingly at Daisy. "I don't like it."

"I'm not for you to like or not like," Daisy grumbled. "But I love Aerwyna like family and I won't let you hurt her!"

He shrugged. "You are a very annoying human."

Daisy shrugged. "So I've been told. But I'm right." She should sing, but was she good enough? *Gift* was so new to her. If she sang would she destroy Kai, but take her guys down with him? She needed to be brave, but the idea of hurting her men made her afraid to use her only real weapon.

Kai chuckled. "Those who've told you that haven't lied, woman. But you might just be what I need to convince my bride to agree."

Daisy shrieked as Kai grabbed her. Chaos broke out around her. Kai had brought guards that embraced the darkness of *gift,* and they used it as a weapon. She could feel River fighting to breathe. He needed to get in the water, away from the one directing power at him. Bayou and Ocean were physically outnumbered as they tried to get to River.

Struggling against Kai's hold, Daisy bit him on the arm. He grunted and backhanded her. She struggled, dazed as he pulled her under the water. Through the bond, she could feel the horror of her men. She held her breath until her chest burned for the need for air. Even with the pendant, her human mind feared letting go of the oxygen in her lungs. What if the necklace didn't work this time?

Kai dragged her downward, deeper and deeper. Finally, she couldn't hold her breath any longer. Pain made her lungs burn. Agony. She had to have air. Her body wouldn't allow her to hold her breath another second.

Daisy tried to send her last thoughts to her guys. Her love. Her regret. She had to suck in a breath, which meant she'd drown if the magic failed her.

Embracing the magic in her necklace, she felt the stone burn against her skin. Closing her eyes, she let the mystical power take over. Death gave her a reprieve.

The pain disappeared. A surge of life-giving oxygen filtered through the gills. Through the bond, she pushed a message to her men that she was okay as her body accepted the water like it was air. The pendant glowed as it floated near her bosom.

Kai widened his eyes. In her head, like a mer, she heard him. *"So, that is how you survived earlier. You have the pendant of Atlantis? Interesting. Which one of your lovers stole it?"*

"None of them! Your bride-to-be gave this to me. She's wonderful. You don't deserve her. She just saved my life!"

Kai grabbed the pendant. It glowed, and he let go of it quickly.

"Killing me won't endear you to your new bride, will it?"

Kai's gaze narrowed. *"You are correct, human.*

Keep it! But I can take your life anytime. For now, you come with me."

Daisy let him drag her further into the depths of the ocean. She wished the plan had been better and she'd had the courage to stick to it.

Chapter Six

Aerwyna struggled against her bonds. That villain, Kai, was never going to be her husband. She wanted to slap him in the face with her tail, but she was currently in human form. He had her under one of the domes. How had he gotten into Atlantis without her father's guards killing him? She knew he was using her to hurt her brother and his Triad. She was almost blind with rage. All she could hope was that Daisy had kept the necklace on.

Her friend was smarter and kinder than most humans she'd encountered. Aerwyna liked her. If River loved the human, she could accept his choice. Maybe their father could even accept it, but if Kai hurt the female then everything was lost. There would never be a truce between her people and the Aegean.

Aerwyna just wanted peace. She'd almost sacrificed her happiness for that simple thing. She'd give anything to make her people happy -- short of marrying Kai. He was a coward, and he'd proven himself a psychopath as well. She struggled against her bonds, but Kai's minions had tied her tightly.

When Kai appeared, dragging Daisy with him, she was both relieved and terrified. If Daisy hadn't been wearing the Jewel of Atlantis, she'd be dead. Aerwyna glanced at her human friend. Daisy widened her eyes when she saw Aerwyna.

"I'm unharmed." Aerwyna sent the thought privately to Daisy.

Together they would fight!

* * *

When Kai swam through some kind of

permeable clear bubble, Daisy had been shocked. Seeing Aerwyna made her feel better.

"Thank God!" Daisy replied. *"You sound normal in my head. Your accent on land is nothing like what I'm hearing now. What can I do to help?"*

"Stay alive, my heart sister," Aerwyna replied. *"And I speak human well!"*

The offended tone brought a sad smile to Daisy's lips. She loved Aerwyna and would fight with everything she had to protect her friend.

"I will!" If Kai tried to kill her, Daisy wasn't going to make it easy for him.

Aerwyna smiled. *"Kai is a worthless mer. Any male who'd hurt females isn't worth his scales. We will fight him. They'll come for you, sister."* Aerwyna sent her love and encouragement with the communication.

"Enough!" Kai roared out loud. "Females! Stop your rude private communications." Disgust hung heavy on him. "If you want the human to live, there is a very simple thing you must do. I no longer require your hand in marriage." Kai motioned for one of the guards. The man brought him a golden disk. "When the princess of Atlantis gives the great seal of the first king to the Agean prince, of her free will, the sea will become the Earth."

Aerwyna struggled against her bonds. "I'll never hand that to you of my own free will!"

Kai reached out and snatched the pendant hanging around Daisy's neck and held it between his fingers. Daisy tried to pull away, but she was afraid of breaking the golden chain and ending her life accidentally. "All I have to do is rip this trinket off her neck and she'll die. Even with air, the pressure at this depth will end her."

"No, don't!" Aerwyna screamed.

Kai grinned. "Humans are so weak. They die so easily in the water. This one seems weaker than most."

Daisy turned to him, narrowing her gaze. "So you think." She managed to elbow Kai in the abdomen, taking him by surprise. He dropped the disk and let go of the pendant.

Daisy stumbled away from him. "Do you like music?"

His guards moved toward her, but she grabbed a spear one of them had dropped when he tried to grab her. She jabbed at the guard, and he leapt back.

Song time. For the first time in her karaoke-loving life, Daisy had no idea what to sing. Her throat tightened. No matter how terrible she was, she'd never had stage fright until this moment. Everything depended on her not screwing up and getting that whole pitch thing perfectly imperfect.

She closed her eyes and focused. *What would Sally do?* If this was the moment, she died she'd honor her best and dearest friend by singing her favorite song. "Come Sail Away" by Styx.

Daisy let those opening piano notes play through her memory. The tinkling in her mind helped her think "high note". She'd never imagined singing to save her life. If they'd been underwater it might not have worked, but there was air in the dome. Closing her eyes, she sucked in a breath of stale air.

"I'm… Sailing… Away…" She let the words out and her voice strained to hit the highest note possible. She kept singing. "Sea…" She jabbed at the guards when then tried to grab her again, stabbing one in the hand when he grabbed for the weapon. "Free…" She took another big breath. "Me…" And drew on her love for her Triad and Aerwyna. "Try to carry on…"

Kai fell to his knees, then slumped to his side,

covering his ears as he convulsed with agony. He grimaced as he flopped helplessly. The guards weren't immune either. They too were immobilized by Daisy's voice. She sang until she was out of lyrics. "Encore!" she sang out loudly before starting all over again. Her lack of talent was working, and she thought about Bayou. He'd said her gift was dark. She couldn't let Kai get away to hurt them, but could she find the kind of darkness she'd need to sing him a fatal note? "Waves…"

Blood ran from Kai's ears to drip on his shoulders.

"Carry on!" Daisy let the violence of the guitar in her head push the notes out. She tried to go darker, but she just couldn't find the level of cruelty she needed to make this power more than immobilizing. How long could she sing? Her throat was beginning to hurt.

"With me… Angels… Skies!" She belted out the lyrics, hitting Kai and his guards with the sonic notes. She thought of Aerwyna being hit by these men and it helped the darkness that fueled whatever she was doing grow. Each word hit more powerfully than a heavyweight boxer.

As her nemesis writhed, guilt surfaced. Her voice faltered for a moment. One of the guards started to stand, fumbling for his weapon. *No.* This was life or death, and if she died, so did the men she loved. Daisy pushed away remorse and forced another high note out.

She kept singing as she used the sharp spearhead to cut through the rope holding Aerwyna. If they left the protected bubble of air, would *gift* work? If they stayed, how long could she keep up singing? Hell, she wasn't even able to swim. Aerwyna might be able to get away, but if Kai caught her, he'd kill her for this.

She sang the first verse of "The Tide is High" by Blondie. All she could do was sing. "Girl…" Her voice cracked. She kept singing. "One…" She tried to draw on the pain in her life. Her darkness. But she was losing steam. "I'm holding on…" But she wasn't holding on. She couldn't keep this up much longer. If she could connect with Bayou's *gift* maybe hers would be dark enough for the song to finish them off.

What if he needed his own energy? She could endanger him by drawing from him as he had her. Without knowing what was happening to her guys she couldn't risk it. She was in a no-win situation. Unshed tears blurred her vision as she tried to sing, but to her horror she was starting to lose her voice. The effort this *gift* stuff made her channel was so intense. She shouldn't be losing her voice so fast.

Using energy, she probably shouldn't spare, she sent her guys all her feelings about failing them. All she could do was keep singing and loving her Triad. But it wasn't enough. She wasn't enough. They deserved better.

Her voice cracked again. The guards began to stir.

* * *

River swam ahead of Ocean and Bayou. He pulled his body through the currents with a desperation he'd never experienced before. He could feel Daisy's fear. A wave of regret hit him. Her regret. She was saying goodbye. He wasn't ready for that. His tail was strong and even if Ocean and Bayou were stronger swimmers, he was putting everything he had into getting to Daisy. He wouldn't let her die alone. He couldn't.

Invisible strands of her love crept through the bond, guiding him to her. He used everything he had to go to her. He sent his father a message that Aerwyna was in trouble, along with where they were, using his private royal family link, a connection he hadn't used in years. He sent all his panic and desperation through the message. There was no way his father would ignore him. He prayed. He hoped. Father was a hard man, but he loved Aerwyna dearly.

River saw the long-abandoned dome below them. Kai had entered Atlantis somehow, and he was using an ancient place of power for his crime against the women River held dearest. Daisy stood with Aerwyna behind her, singing.

Even through the water and dome he felt the pain of his mate's *gift*. Her power was ebbing, but she still had a fearsome darkness that made what she was doing possible. Kai should be dead, but Daisy was no killer. Everything about his mate blew him away. How had he been blessed that this amazing woman as his -- theirs?

He looked back. Bayou was passing Ocean and gaining on him. Something intense in his friend's eyes told him how close to giving up Daisy must be. Bayou's darkness must have a connection to Daisy's.

He and Bayou swam neck and neck to the dome. Bayou overtook him to be the first one to enter. As the air hit Bayou, his tail morphed into legs and he rolled till he was standing next to Daisy. He'd keep them together when they needed strength most. As much as River wanted to be the hero, he couldn't. He was suffering from the sonic pitch as much as the enemy. Why hadn't they grabbed the earplugs? They'd all panicked at the wrong moments.

Bayou grabbed Daisy's arm and River knew he was pushing *gift* into her. Her voice rose, and pain slammed into River. Every muscle in his body ached and his head throbbed. Daisy realized mermen didn't have pockets. They also had to have freaked out when she was grabbed. The whole plan was for nothing. They didn't have ear protection, and both River and Ocean hit the dome to collapse on the ground in tortured agony at the very moment they entered the air-filled room. Her notes rose even higher, and River knew even Bayou could die, but he didn't let go of Daisy. He didn't relent as he pushed his darkness into their mate her *gift* built on what Bayou gave her.

Aerwyna covered Bayou's ears with her hands as Daisy sang. River managed to crawl to Ocean, who was unconscious, and covered Ocean's ears as the song stole his own ability to stay with them. River wanted to be there for his dearest ones, but he couldn't.

* * *

River opened his eyes, blinking into the light. Was he alive? "Daisy!" His voice was rusty and his mouth dry.

Aerwyna laid her hand on his shoulder. "All is well, Brother. Daisy is safe."

"What -- what happened?" He looked around. "Where am I?"

"You're home. Have been gone so long you no longer recognize the palace of Atlantis?" Aerwyna chuckled. "Your mate is stronger than you males give her credit for. She needed Bayou's darkness because she couldn't find her own abyss, but they didn't need to destroy Kai. Father arrived with the army. Both she and Bayou collapsed the moment they no longer needed to keep Kai and his guards immobilized."

River's heart gave a pained beat. "I need to see them."

"They need rest, as do you. They'll recover, and have had the finest physician in the city care for them.

Daisy doesn't remember much. Bayou is suffering such an intense migraine they've been giving him medicine to make him sleep. We've done what we can. Bayou is in your room. Father had kept it for you, but I insisted we give him a space with your energy to help his recovery. Ocean has been banned from going to him, which has made him crazy, but he also needs to heal before he goes to heal others. I've been assured you will all recover in time. The healing will coming easier when your Triad and mate are reunited to give each other comfort, but the doctor is convinced you will each need to find your own strength before you try to share with one another."

"I need to see Daisy," River insisted. "I just need to see that she is okay with my own eyes."

"Daisy is awake. I'm keeping her in my quarters until you males get your heads together. She'll try to fix all your brokenness if you go to her before the three of you get your pieces put back together. Father wants to see you when you're up to it."

River grunted. "So that he can yell at me?" He looked at the ancient murals on the walls of the room.

Aerwyna shook her head. "He will not yell. Father is not one to easily admit wrongdoing. Please be kind to him. He is no longer against your choice of human mate. He didn't know that the right human can find *gift*. None of us knew. When he learned how Daisy took down Kai, he was very impressed. With Kai as a hostage, we've signed the first real peace treaty in a thousand years. Your mate has given Atlantis the one thing we really needed, peace. Daisy is a heroine to our people." Aerwyna shook her head, grinning. "He gave her a tour of the garden and they've spent a long time talking this morning."

"Is she okay?" River sat up. "Father didn't scold

her?"

Aerwyna rolled her eyes. "I think you should be more worried for Father. She is a sharp-tongued woman, but that's what you need. I've never seen him so impressed with a human before. He forgave me for giving her the Jewel of Atlantis and even gifted me a new shell for my hair as a thank you for my foresight. He gifted your woman our mother's favorite hair comb, citizenship and a title. Your Daisy is Lady of the Land, and welcome in the currents now. I guess you'd better be good to her because she could stay down here and have any young lord very excited to create a union."

River glared at his sister. "No one, other than our Triad, will be claiming Daisy."

Aerwyna chuckled. "She's made that very clear. Father did tell her she could do better than you."

"Father!" River huffed gruffly.

Aewyna nodded. "And Daisy wasn't very lady-like in her response. Before Father laughed, I thought I'd die of fright for her."

River grimaced. "I can imagine. He must be getting soft in his old age."

"Oh, dear brother, don't let anyone besides me hear you say that!"

River nodded. "I'm just surprised."

"As was I. But I told father how caring your mate is. When he saw and felt her power, he declared that she is surely of siren stock. He's convinced she's not fully human. And after what Bayou did, Father has given him and Ocean both clemencies. No one, not even him, will dare call them traitors again."

River took his sister's hand. "If I ask Father to make you his heir, will you accept that responsibility?"

Aerwyna gaped at him. "Brother?"

"You should rule after Father. You're the right one to be heir to the throne. You would be the best for our people."

"But Brother --"

"Sister, you are the one who has the heart to rule. You have always been the one to have the best interest of our people at heart."

Aerwyna bowed her head to him. "If you truly do not wish to rule, I will do so in your stead."

"I'm ready to see Father," River lied.

Chapter Seven

Father sat on the throne, his long gray hair tied back by golden cords. He was dressed in ceremonial vestments in the house colors of aqua and gold. River wondered what the occasion was as he arrived to bow before his father. "I've been told you wish to speak with me."

Father stood. "Clear the room. I would speak with my son in private."

The lords and advisors shuffled out quietly. A few wore annoyed expressions, but none dared argue.

"River, I've wronged you and your Triad. Kai confessed he tried to make Aerwyna hand him the seal. He'd have used the magic to cause Atlantis to rise. I'd believed that spell was lost to time. If your human hadn't been there and used her most wretched singing voice to stop him, the city would have risen to displace the sea. It would have caused another great cataclysm of tsunamis that would have decimated the human world and destroyed our city. Kai's people alone would have ruled both the land and the sea. Daisy saved everything with the strength of your Triad and your sister's pilfered gift. I just wanted to tell you that I am sorry."

"Father, please --"

Father held up his hand to silence him. "No, my dear son, I've seen your kindness as a weakness instead of seeing how strong love can make a leader. Your Triad and mate are welcome in our city, but I am hoping you'll make it your home again. You've been away too long."

River's throat tightened. His father had never

spoken to him as kindly as he was right now, but River couldn't commit to returning. "I -- I'm not sure we are *all* ready."

"Son, the people are restless to see their prince. They fear what might happen to my heir outside the safety of the kingdom. I, too, share those fears." Desperation gave weight to the king's words.

"I understand. I also know that you have a far better heir who is much more knowledgeable about how to rule when you're gone. Consider changing the laws of succession and giving Aerwyna my place on the throne."

His father widened his eyes. "You would give up your legacy?" Hurt and anger flashed across Father's face.

"No, I would be gifting Aerwyna the legacy she has earned. She is good with our people, and she's studied the ancient laws and magic. She's forgotten more about our history than I have ever learned. She is the princess Atlantis deserves as queen. I am not giving up my people or my love for my family below the water, but I would give everything to care for my family above the water the way I choose." He stood quietly, watching his father contemplate his words.

Father scowled, and then his expression changed, softening when he looked into River's eyes. "You never longed for power. I thought that would make you a ruler who would strive for peace. But you're right, your sister has worked diligent at my side to help rule our people. She has earned the throne. I will see what can be done, but I cannot promise you that you won't be called to rule.

"If I do give her the throne, you must give me your word you will not abandon her for the world of the landers. She will need you to take part in ceremonial duties and show your support to help the people accept her as queen. Now that your Triad has been given pardons and your human can survive here, you have no excuses. Please, show the people their prince has not forgotten his duty to them."

River bowed deeply. When he straightened, he saw his father's sad smile and it broke his heart a little. "Thank you, Father."

"As I have said, don't thank me until I've changed a law that has stood unchallenged for three thousand years." Father chuckled darkly. "You've never been one to ask for small favors. Go to your family."

River nodded. "Father, I love and respect you. Please don't doubt that." He pretended not to notice the moisture in the corners of his father's eyes.

* * *

"Is this really necessary?" Daisy complained as River kept her eyes covered while Bayou and Ocean guided her down the path. Atlantis had been such an amazing experience; she really didn't think they could show her anything that could top the wonders she'd already witnessed.

"Ready," River asked.

"I guess so," Daisy replied. She opened her eyes to the most beautiful thing she'd ever seen. Stones shimmered with such a beautiful glow that it caused Daisy's throat to tighten. Her heart ached in response.

"This is the Shrine of the First Triad," Ocean said. "It will have an effect on us far greater than most. Is it too intense for you?"

Daisy hadn't even realized she was crying. The shrine shimmered with a light that was a color she couldn't exactly describe. The massive stones shifted with a roar of noise. She took a step back and glanced up at Bayou.

He took her hand. "We're being welcomed." His voice was rougher than usual and there was huskiness in his tone.

"Welcomed?" she looked back to where the sparkling brightness seemed to leap around the ancient stones.

Ocean put his arm around her. "This is the most sacred moment for a Triad of our kind. We've been found worthy."

"How do those lights know anything about us, or even begin to judge our worth? Are you sure this is really something good?" Daisy fought for the courage to enter as she watched River walk between the stones.

River stood silently as the illumination rolled over him from head to toe. The brightness grew as he remained between the stones. He closed his eyes and Daisy held her breath.

When River's beautiful eyes opened there was a shimmer of unshed tears. "We are chosen to enter. The first Triad's spirits dwell here, and our hearts have been judged."

Daisy didn't like the idea of some random force judging her. She frowned. One of the lights on River's chest floated away and toward her. The entity reminded her of a firefly. She forced herself not to flinch as it landed on her arm. She watched it brighten. A warmth filled her in the same way she experienced Ocean's gift. Bayou kept holding her hand and Ocean took her other arm in his as they made their way through the opening.

A fount of water sprang up carving a timeless crevice in a huge moss-covered rock that was decorated with numerous carvings. Daisy couldn't read them but seeing them filled her with peace. "What are they?"

"It's the story of the first Triad and their mate," River explained. "We are being offered a blessing."

"What kind of blessing?" Daisy asked, skeptical.

"Take off your clothing," Bayou whispered in her ear. "And find out."

"What? Here? Now?" Heat burned Daisy's cheeks.

"Yes." Ocean let go of her hand and pulled his shirt over his head. "Here and now. I promise this is going to be something you'll never forget."

She rolled her eyes. "I bet you say that to all the girls."

Bayou chuckled, and Ocean shot him a dark look. River disrobed, and Ocean was soon equally naked. Daisy squeezed Bayou's hand.

He squeezed back. "You can do this. Please. I swear it's real. We're meant to be here together."

"It just feels weird getting naked in a sacred space. I feel like I'm going to defile something. River's dad just started to like me. I'm sure the last thing the king of Atlantis needs is a human going around sexing it up in all the shrines under the dome."

River made a sound that was half of a chuckle and half of a groan. "The last thing I want is to think about my father at a time like this. I swear to you, this space is meant for lovemaking. Triad might not be as common anymore, but it's respected. I've heard legends about the magic of the spirits here and how a Triad who is welcomed leaves changed forever."

Daisy didn't know if she wanted to be changed forever, but she did know she wanted her guys to be happy. Right now, they all looked happy -- and horny. Bayou had let go of her hand when River was talking, and he was already out of his clothing.

"When in Rome..." Daisy shrugged. "Or Atlantis, in this case, do as the Atlanteans do."

"Right now we want to do you, sand dragon," Ocean replied. There was a tension in his voice, and he stroked his cock. "But I think you're overdressed."

Bayou moved closer to her. "Can I help you with that?"

Daisy nodded mutely. Her pussy suddenly ached with the need to be filled. And filled. And filled. He gently unzipped her hoodie and pulled it off her shoulders, letting it fall to the ground. Then he took the hem of her shirt and pulled it over her head.

Ocean approached her from the other side, and he put his hand on the zipper of her jeans. "Is this okay?"

Daisy nodded, and Ocean unbuttoned her fly before pushing the denim off her hips. River knelt at her feet. He took one of her feet in his hands, Bayou and Ocean both standing behind her making sure she was steady.

"Let me," River said as he untied her running shoes and carefully removed them and her socks one foot at a time. He kissed the top of her foot. "We are yours, today and always."

She stepped out of the pants, her stomach fluttering and her heart beating a little faster. Love for these men made her throat tighten. River stood and took her in his arms. His lips descended on hers, the awkwardness of sex shrine left, and her desire consumed her with the sensation of his kiss. Sighing, she let his lips lead hers in a dance against his very practiced mouth. Daisy let sensuality wash over her in waves of wet heat. His kiss alone made her want so much more. She'd never been so ready in her life.

For just a moment she wondered if it was some

magic in the shrine, but then Bayou's fingers found her clit and her knees buckled. Without conscious thought she wrapped her arms around River's neck, and he deepened the kiss. He pulled her against him and his hand slid down her back to clutch her buttocks. She gasped against his lips as he gave her ass a firm squeeze.

She ignited with his touch, moaning into his kiss, and he growled against her lips, pressing his naked body against her a delicious slide. When she looked into his eyes she saw heat there as well as the darkness of his desire. He moved his mouth to the tender skin under her ear, kissing and sucking. Delighted shivers ran down her spine and she twined her fingers in the dark mass of his thick hair.

Bayou kept his fingers busy. If Ocean hadn't been holding her up, she'd have collapsed. Her legs shook. Drunk with desire, she reveled in the musky scent of her men. River's mouth traveled down to her breast. She cried out with a gasp, her breath coming in little puffs as he found her nipple.

Ocean's lips skimmed her right shoulder.

"Let's lay her down," Bayou said. "Our girl looks about ready to fall over."

As if on cue, an organic platform of some sort of soft plant life rose near the trickling spring. River picked her up and carried her over to the offering from the shrine. She gazed up at her men as they crowed around her. "I feel like an offering to your gods," she said softly, but her tone lacked the humor she'd been striving for.

"You are," Ocean said. "When we make you cum, your screams of pleasure will be all the worship they need."

"Just as long as they don't expect a good sex-face.

I'm sure mine looks terrible."

Bayou pinched her nipple. "Your sex face looks fine to me. I guess I need to see it again to be sure. What should we do about that?" He pinched harder.

Daisy gasped and bucked. "More."

Bayou chuckled. "You smell so fucking good right now. You want more?" He leaned down and took her other nipple in his mouth, biting. Pain and pleasure mingled.

She held him to her breast. "Don't stop," she begged in a whisper.

He wrapped his arms around her and straddled her prone body as he worked her breast with wildness. There was nothing gentle in the carnality with which he devoured her. Daisy loved it.

Ocean parted her legs. "Look at her glisten. Damn, she's as beautiful as those lights. She's so ready. I think our girl needs a good fucking."

"She does," River agreed. "I'll want to feel your hard cock against my hand while I rub her needy little clit. Fuck her good and slow." He pressed down on her mound as he rubbed her clit fast and hard.

Daisy cried out as Ocean entered her. Bayou was still on top of her, working her breasts with his mouth. He took turns, first the right and then the left, until she was blind with need. "I'm so close," she breathed. "Please. Please."

Ocean picked up his speed and she hit her peak, shattering hard, her pussy convulsed around his cock. "Daisy!" Ocean called out as he came.

Her pussy was still quivering as he pulled out. "My turn." River chuckled. And then he slipped inside her. Her desire kindled again, and she squeezed her eyes tight riding the wave of another orgasm.

Bayou was kissing her face and chest now:

breasts, lips, cheeks, eyelids, forehead. "Mine. Mine," he whispered as he dragged his lips over her skin. "Mine."

Another tsunami of desire crashed down and she choked out a cry as her muscles tightened against the cock inside her. Mindlessly, she came again. River had staying power, and it wasn't until her screams became whimpers that she felt the heat of his seed fill her.

She blinked open her eyes as she came back to reality. Bayou gazed down into her face watching her. "Your sex face is beautiful. Our gods are blessed." He kissed the tip of her nose.

"It's your turn," she whispered.

"Are you sure you're up for more?" A shadow of uncertainty passed over Bayou's expression.

"I feel empty without you inside me, too."

He smiled down at her so lovingly her heart hurt. He'd come so far from the moody, angry man she'd first met. "Then I think it's only right you get to be in control." He moved so that he was no longer straddling her and lay next to her on the natural bed. "Ride me, Daisy."

"Let me help build you back." River helped her to her knees and positioned her over Bayou as he stood behind her and rubbed her clit with one hand while cupping a breast with his other. "Take your time and your pleasure."

Bayou gazed up at her. "I'm all yours."

Daisy bit her lip and closed her eyes against the desire River's hands stirred. Ocean ran his fingers through her hair. *Gift* made her shiver. He'd used it to comfort her often, but this was the first time he'd used it sexually. She carefully pressed down, and the head of Bayou's cock slipped inside.

He hissed between his teeth as she lowered

herself until his thick cock was surrounded by her pussy. Then she began to move until she found their rhythm. Everything felt good, right. Her men all worked together with her at the center of this beautiful physical display of love and commitment. She let the vast sea of need and joy crash in waves around her as her orgasm rolled to its zenith. "I love you all…" Daisy managed the words around a moan as she collapsed on Bayou's chest.

He grunted softly with release as he wrapped his arms around her. "Forever," he whispered. "Promise you'll never walk away."

She turned her head so she could see his face. "Never. You're stuck with me."

"Good." Relief lived in that single word. "Good." He held her tighter.

Daisy was exhausted. She'd never imagined sex with these men could be more exciting than seeing the city of Atlantis or more exhilarating than saving the world. She allowed her eyes to drift closed. "I hope snoring in a sacred shrine isn't a problem."

The last sound she heard as she drifted off was River's chuckle.

Epilogue

Six Months Later

Wind bit into Daisy as she watched the island come into view. It was good to be home. *Home*. This was her home now. Her mates were her world. In the six months since they'd saved the world her life had settled into a lovely peaceful pace. She patted her growing middle. She was really going to raise a child with them. As crazy as it was, she was going to be the mother of a little mermaid in a few more months. As hard as it was to wrap her head around it, somehow all three of the men really were her baby's father. Mer biology was something she didn't need to know the specifics about to understand. This was the magic of that special night under the sea in the shrine of the First Triad.

Ocean sat down next to her and put his hand over hers where it rested on their child. "How did your appointment go?" She heard a touch of sadness in the question.

"You know even if I'm River's fiancé for the sake of the show, you can come to an appointment or two if you want. This is just as much your baby as his."

Through the bond, she experienced his happiness at the acknowledgement. "I know I can, but everything off the island is a lie. I want every moment with you and our baby to be the truth. It would be too hard for me not to do something obvious and give us away. It's probably for the best that we decided River gets to play human husband because there's no way I'd be able to let you experience labor without using *gift*."

"It would freak out the doctors if you started doing the screaming while I just laid there watching you." She chuckled.

Ocean rolled his eyes. "I'd try to be dignified about it."

Now Daisy laughed. "I don't plan to be."

She felt the peace he pushed into her through *gift*. "I know you're nervous, but you're strong. We've found you the best hospital and doctor. The water birth will help our princess ease into the world too. Mer births are normally much easier than human ones. The doctors will be concerned about the gestation being shorter, but when she's healthy they'll just assume they miscalculated."

Daisy nodded. "Today Dr. Marx commented that she's going to be a big baby because she's growing so fast."

"Don't let that worry you. They just expect you to stay pregnant a little longer than you will."

"Did you come to pick us up just to make sure I wasn't scared? You shouldn't use *gift* with me as much as you do. When the baby is born you can't use it on the baby except for emergencies. Please promise me."

He sighed. "I know. She'll have to learn how to regulate her emotions without her father's constant interference. I just want to take care of you both."

Daisy leaned closer to him and brushed his cheek with her lips. "You're a good mate. You'll be an excellent father. Are you scared?"

"Not as much as Bayou."

Daisy nodded. Bayou was constantly researching everything that could possibly go wrong with the pregnancy and children. Their child not only going to be half human or whatever percentage she got considering all three of them had impregnated her, but their baby had been conceived surrounded by the most sacred magic in Atlantis. It wasn't a surprise that he was a nervous wreck. She honestly was too.

Ocean brightened. "I did have another reason for the trip. I have good news."

"Is that what I felt right around noon? I've been smiling all day."

He winked. "I tried to hold back. I bet River has guessed. Come with me and I'll tell you both."

"That sounds great," Daisy said as he helped her stand. She followed him to the wheel where River was focused on steering the boat.

He turned as they came into the wheelhouse and smiled. "Did you come in here to give me a long talk about safety when taking Daisy anywhere? Bayou beat you to it before we left this morning."

Daisy shook her head. "Nope. Ocean has good news."

"Renewal is my favorite word," River said.

Ocean swore softly then glanced apologetically at Daisy's belly. "Trying to surprise a mind reader is pointless. Yes, the show was renewed. Editing used the footage you managed to shoot along with some stuff cut from earlier in the season, and those engagement interviews really heighten the drama." He turned to her. "Thank you for playing along with us on making it look like River's focus is slipping and we're all having tension because of his new fiancé. If they only knew!" He looked at River again. "No delays and the ads are going to be great."

"Not pointless," Daisy said. "Thoughtful and sweet. Ocean, the baby can't hear you, so get all your swearing out of your system now." She paused. "Or can she? Will she have *gift*? Does she have *gift*?" Worry and a sense of unpreparedness sent a chill through

Daisy. She shivered.

"She probably will. But only time will tell. Mer *gift* emerges typically around puberty, but she's special so I have no idea what we can expect. Just don't sing her a lullaby. I'm sure it'll be like parenting any human child."

Daisy whacked his arm half-playfully and half-vengefully. "Great, best-case scenario we have puberty and magic happening at the same time. What a terrifying hot mess we have to look forward to." She paused. "If it's not worse and we have a hocus-pocus baby. Either way, there are zero parenting books that cover this."

Ocean kissed Daisy's forehead. "*Gift* isn't hocus pocus, you know that."

"I'm just hangry."

He glared at River. "You didn't feed her?"

"I fed her twice," River grumbled.

"You know I'm still here, right? Also, I can feed myself. I just get peckish more often these days."

"I promise to feed you as soon as we're home if you promise to never call *gift* hocus pocus again." Ocean crossed his arms over his chest.

Daisy grinned. "I won't. That was rude of me. I know how you feel because I feel how you feel." She gave him a fake pout. "I'm sorry for what I said when I was hungry."

He tipped her chin up. "Being cute to get out of trouble is unfair." He kissed the tip of her nose.

"I don't know anything about hocus pocus, but I do know a thing or two about magic," River said drawing her attention back to him.

"Are you calling *gift* magic?" Daisy glanced at Ocean to see if he was disgruntled with the comparison. "Because we all know it's nature and religion and life. Feeling it through you guys is kind of incredible."

River snickered. "No. I'm not talking about *gift*. I'm talking about you, mate. You're the magic. You're all the magic I'll ever need or want."

She went over to him and brushed her lips over his before getting out of his way so he could keep steering safely. Even all the way on the island she felt a stirring of awareness of Bayou. He was thinking about them, her most specifically. And love just poured into her soul.

They were magic. Her mermen were the hocus to her pocus. She might not be the maid for these mermen anymore, but she was mate for them and mad for her mermen. All she wanted from the time she woke up to the time she went to bed was to make them happy. They helped her live her best life. Joy and contentment filled her. There'd be waves and rough seas, but for now, she'd just enjoy the smooth sailing.

Ashlynn Monroe

Ashlynn Monroe is a busy working mom. She loves her kids and family. Her greatest joy is creating stories to entertain others, and she hopes they bring a little more romance into the world. She's been writing since her teens for her own enjoyment but decided in her thirties to share her imagination with readers. Ashlynn enjoys biking, camping, reading, video games, and filling her home and life with love. If she's not working or chasing children, you can find her daydreaming up her next tale of romance.

Ashlynn at Changeling: changelingpress.com/ashlynn-monroe-a-166

Changeling Press LLC

Contemporary Action Adventure, Sci-Fi, Steampunk, Dark Fantasy, Urban Fantasy, Paranormal, and BDSM Romance available in e-book, audio, and print format at ChangelingPress.com – MC Romance, Werewolves, Vampires, Dragons, Shapeshifters and Horror -- Tales from the edge of your imagination.

Where can I get Changeling Press Books?

Changeling Press e-books are available at ChangelingPress.com, Amazon, Apple Books, Barnes & Noble, Kobo, Smashwords, and other online retailers, including Everand Subscription and Kobo Subscription Services. Print books are available at Amazon, Barnes and Noble, and by ISBN special order through your local bookstores.

ChangelingPress.com